Praise for
DANIEL COLDSTAR
THE BETRAYER

"What an epic space adventure and fun sci-fi read!
I love it!"— **Dr. S. Alan Stern**, planetary scientist, coauthor
of *Chasing New Horizons: Inside the Epic First Mission to
Pluto*, and leader of NASA's New Horizons mission to
Pluto and the Kuiper Belt

"Underneath all the whizbang, this is ultimately a story
about friendship and family, and who doesn't need that in
tough times? A satisfying sequel!"— **Taran Matharu**, *New
York Times* bestselling author of the Summoner series

"A sci-fi adventure that's equal parts mystery, comedy,
and action, *Daniel Coldstar: The Betrayer* will keep pages
flipping at warp speed."— **Kim Tomsic**, winner of the
Crystal Kite Award for *The 11:11 Wish*

"*Daniel Coldstar: The Betrayer* is a binge-worthy read
that slingshots from one electrifying scene to the next.
Thoughtful, well written, inventive, but most of all, pure
fun."— **Rob Vlock**, author of the Sven Carter series

"Packed with action and rip-roaring adventure, this
space saga is sure to appeal to sci-fi readers of all ages!"
— **Gareth Wronski**, author of *Holly Farb and the
Princess of the Galaxy*

"Thrills, surprises, laughs, and genuine heart—this is the
rare sequel that's more than worthy of its predecessor.
The Daniel Coldstar books are perfect for young readers
getting their feet wet in sci-fi!"— **Katie Slivensky**, author of
The Countdown Conspiracy and *The Seismic Seven*

"Action-packed, thought-provoking, and FUN—this is science fiction at its best."— **Jarrett Lerner**, author of the Enginerds series

Praise for
DANIEL COLDSTAR
THE RELIC WAR

"Sci-fi has never been so much fun. I loved it!"
— **Eoin Colfer**, bestselling author of *Artemis Fowl*

"A breathless adventure full of surprise twists, daring escapes, awesome tech, and sinister conspiracies!"
— **Joel Ross**, author of *Beast & Crown*

"Outrageously creative."— *Kirkus Reviews*

"There's more than a touch of Star Wars sensibility here. An effective gateway through which to lure space-addicted middle-schoolers from movies into books."
— *Bulletin of the Center for Children's Books*

"[An] action-packed journey [with] interesting themes on truth, power, and wisdom. [A] zany outer space adventure. Sure to be a hit for sci-fi readers who love a wild romp."
— *School Library Journal*

DANIEL COLDSTAR

THE BETRAYER

STEL PAVLOU

HARPER
An Imprint of HarperCollinsPublishers

Also by Stel Pavlou
Daniel Coldstar: The Relic War

Daniel Coldstar #2: The Betrayer
Copyright © 2019 by Stel Pavlou
For information address HarperCollins Children's
Books, a division of HarperCollins Publishers, 195 Broadway, New York, NY
10007.
www.harpercollinschildrens.com

Library of Congress Cataloging-in-Publication Data

Names: Pavlou, Stel, author.
Title: The betrayer / Stel Pavlou.
Description: First edition. | New York, NY : Harper, an imprint of
 HarperCollinsPublishers, [2019] | Series: Daniel Coldstar ; #2 | Summary:
 Daniel and his friends continue their mission as Truth Seekers, fighting and
 improvising their way through an intergalactic space adventure.
Identifiers: LCCN 2018061526 | ISBN 9780062126092 (hardcover)
Subjects: | CYAC: Life on other planets--Fiction. | Adventure and adventurers--
 Fiction. | Orphans--Fiction. | Science fiction.
Classification: LCC PZ7.1.P38542 Bet 2019 | DDC [Fic]--dc23 LC record available
 at https://lccn.loc.gov/2018061526

Typography by Joel Tippie
19 20 21 22 23   PC/LSCH   10 9 8 7 6 5 4 3 2 1

First Edition

For my mother, Maureen

CONTENTS

DANIEL COLDSTAR
THE BETRAYER

Somewhen in the Exodussic Age . . .

1

A MAP OF HOPE

Nobody came here by choice. Now Daniel Coldstar knew why.

In the steamy Death Jungles of Oota Mheen, fifteen species of plant were poisonous to the touch. Thirty-seven types of bug could either sting, bite, or burrow their way into his brain. In every direction, massive tree trunks stood twisted together, while creeping vines strangled them, reaching all the way up to the branches overhead and forming impenetrable walls of black vegetation. Vicious eyes bored into him from creatures who sat crouched, hidden in the dense foliage, waiting to pounce.

Everything was out to get him.

Daniel waded ankle-deep through lead-colored water, struggling to pull his feet from the sucking mud, when he heard a heavy *splash!*

Out of the corner of his eye he saw something slug-colored slither out of a nightmare and into the swamp.

What was that?

Waves rippled out toward Daniel. Poisonous algae swirled around his legs: akahana, toxic to humans and the best way to get blood to squirt from your eyeballs if swallowed. A minor inconvenience compared to fighting off an attack, but if that thing pulled him down into the water?

Maybe better to avoid a fight altogether.

Daniel held his breath. He stood perfectly still and waited for the creature to pass, sweat trickling down the back of his neck. The thick, heavy air burned in his throat—

Roaaar-kha-kha . . . ! Roaaar-kha-kha . . . !

The howl of a Jaranjar, what the locals called tiger-apes, echoed through distant treetops. Daniel sure hoped it wasn't coming this way, because that was all he needed right now.

Where did that thing in the water go?

There, its back arching as it surfaced. It headed in the other direction.

Daniel let himself take a breath.

"Maybe Nails was right," he said to himself. "Maybe this *is* a trap." He glanced around, wondering what options he had left. If he went back now, Ben and Ionica and all the other Truth Seekers would never know he'd been gone, but he'd never get his answer.

Waving his hand in an arc in front of his body, Daniel called up his holographic display. A map quickly projected out in the air around him. Ahead and behind, a series of glowing orbs snaked their way through the undergrowth. Red, showing where he had been; blue, showing where he needed to go.

He trudged on, making his way up onto drier land where brittle twigs snapped underfoot; oblivious to a small metal flipper silently reaching out from the bushes.

It tapped him on the leg.

Daniel instinctively pulled his hand up, readying his Aegis—the weapon of a Truth Seeker. Ancient and powerful, a relic crafted by an unknown alien intelligence and forged from a single starflake, a crystal formed at the heart of a sun. The weapon vibrated faintly on his chest, listening to Daniel's thoughts, eager to bend all matter and energy into a powerful shield around its master.

But it was a false alarm.

"Will you stop doing that?" Daniel snapped. "I could have blasted you to pieces."

A few feet away, a nervous mechanical penguin bobbed from one webbed foot to the other. Its tritanium beak snapped shut like a steel trap while its crest of yellow light-wire feathers twitched disapprovingly over each eye.

"Don't give me that look," said Daniel. "It's not my fault Astrid didn't program you for speech."

The anatom, a cyborg fusion of machine and artificial life, puffed out his chest and extended his neck.

"Jasper . . . ," Daniel said, "I'm warning you—"

Jasper tilted his head, then gagged.

"Ugh, that's revolting!" Daniel agreed, cupping a hand

over his nose. "I think something died."

Jasper waddled off in search of the source. Humming.

Great anatom design, Astrid, Daniel thought. *Can't speak Mendese, but can hold a tune.*

Astrid Always. Always Astrid, always right. That was how she described herself. Constantly. She had a truly brilliant mind wrapped in an irritating personality. No doubt she had good reason for how she had programmed Jasper. She had just neglected to tell anyone what that reason was.

Daniel hadn't known it at the time, but the first moment he met Astrid, she was already hard at work building Jasper aboard the *Equinox.* Of course, Daniel had had other concerns back then. Like his damaged traveling companion, an anatom named Hex. The rat had needed an entirely new exosuit and wound up wearing a mishmash of spare parts.

In retrospect, Daniel wished Hex had remained a rat. Maybe it would have made it easier to identify him as the betrayer he had turned out to be. Daniel hadn't quite trusted anatoms since then. Not even Jasper.

"I'm not sure this is a good idea," Daniel warned, reluctantly tagging along behind the penguin until their way was blocked by a dense mesh of leaves and vines that seemed to come in at least three different shades of black.

Daniel had never stepped foot on a planet that orbited a red dwarf before now. Here on Oota Mheen, the vegetation had evolved to absorb every ray of the star's weak sunlight by turning black instead of green. It looked as though shadows had become living things. It took some getting used to, not only because it looked so strange, but because—

The leaves rustled. Something was coming toward them. Something big, something so huge that it didn't care one bit about the supposedly impenetrable barrier of dense foliage.

Please don't be a Jaranjar. Please . . .

Its muzzle emerged first, a gigantic mouth set wide beneath wet, twitching nostrils. Forcing its way through, the rest of its gigantic head soon followed. Its face contorted as though it was uncomfortable. Then it farted.

"Eww, *really?*" Daniel now had *both* hands cupped over his nose. "This is where you went? What did I teach you about going downwind? No wonder that thing back there decided to go for a swim. Thanks a lot!"

For his part, Alice the Hammertail looked very pleased with himself.

Daniel tugged on Alice's reins, coaxing the massive trabasaur out into the open. Trabasaurs came in all sorts of shapes and sizes. In class, Daniel had learned that these work beasts were originally genetically engineered to resemble the dinosaurs of olden times. Alice had a gigantic spiked hammer on the end of his tail, perfect for smashing things.

Alice liked to smash things.

"You couldn't go a little farther away? I told you to drink more water, but no, you had to get backed up for three days."

Jasper angrily raised a flipper, eager to chop Alice in the knee. Alice raised an irritated foot, ready to crush the annoying little robot.

"Cut it out, the pair of you!" Daniel scolded. "We're not done here yet. Come on!"

They trekked on for another hour, listening to the buzz of insects and the chirp of things that kind of looked like birds. They had wings but they didn't have feathers. They had what looked like beaks, except they weren't; they were teeth all nested together, and Daniel only found this out when one of them dived at him and snapped at his face.

Though Daniel would never admit to it, having Alice here was a comfort. Not even a fresh mind wipe had managed to break the bond the two of them had formed back in the Sinja's relic mines.

The relic mines. Where he'd unearthed the Aegis now attached to his chest, and won his freedom. That was over a year ago—had it really been so long? So much had happened since then.

Daniel took what he thought was going to be another careful step, but Alice gently nudged him out of the way.

The unfurled drab green petals of a trap-bloom lay stretched out on the forest floor. These plants were carnivorous, sitting openmouthed on the ground for as long as it took for something tasty to wander through and then—*snap!* Lunchtime.

Daniel gave the Hammertail a thankful pat on the shoulder before checking the map one last time. "This is it," he said, "right over there."

He took a deep breath and hesitated.

Either he was about to uncover the first major clue in figuring out who he was and where he came from. Or he had been lied to. Again.

The trees parted like curtains as Alice forced his way through. Cautiously, Daniel kept one step behind him, and Jasper behind him, picking their way over the warped stumps until the three of them emerged together into a clearing bowled at the foot of a steep hill.

It took a moment for Daniel to truly grasp the enormity of what he was seeing. At first it looked like a natural formation, a rocky outcropping covered in growth. But looking closer, he could see gaping black holes that used to be windows. Trees grew between exposed metal ribs, tall enough to hide much of the hull. Moss cascaded down the letters emblazoned across its bow.

This was a starship, lying on its broken back, engines in the air.

This is it! This is really it!

Whoever had sent him the map had been telling the truth.

There *was* a crashed ship on Oota Mheen, and its name was *Coldstar*.

2

THE MYSTERIOUS SHIP

Muscles rippled along Alice's back as he heaved at the vines Daniel had tied to the trabasaur's saddle. Thick festoons of vegetation slowly peeled away from the ship to expose its rotting hull.

The starliner moaned miserably from deep within as though the creepers had been the only thing holding it together. Daniel was going to find a way inside this ship even if he had to tear a hole—

Alice lurched forward and the aging metal screamed.

The great tangle of vines snapped taut. Then a large strip of twisted hull metal tore away from the wreckage and tumbled to the ground, leaving behind a gaping hole big enough for Daniel to climb through—if he could get up there.

"That works," Daniel remarked, chopping the vines from where he'd tied them to Alice's back. He pulled a tasty treat from his utility belt. Tawanga, a type of dried fruit and fried bugs shaped into chewy sticks that he'd picked up on his travels, had quickly become Alice's favorite snack.

Daniel peered up at the hole in the side of the wreck, which sat two or three floors up. An easy jump with his Aegis, if only he knew what he would be jumping into.

Jasper had the same concern. Protectively blocking Daniel's way with his flipper, he opened his beak and shot a grappling hook up to the branch nearest the opening. The whir of a tiny motor was the only sound the anatom made as he respooled the microwire line and rose up into the air, mouth first.

Dangling in front of the hole, Jasper shone a light inside.

"What do you see?" Daniel called up, which was dumb, because no matter what Jasper saw he couldn't tell Daniel about it. He couldn't talk! "Never mind . . . !"

Jasper swung back and forth for a moment, building momentum until—*click!* He disengaged the grappling hook and leapt into the dark.

A loud clank echoed out from the opening. Followed by more clanks, a squawk, and a couple of bat-like things flying off to find a new home.

Moments later an F-light went on.

Then Jasper's familiar humming started up again.

"I guess that means it's okay," Daniel said, heading back

11

to Alice to retrieve his backpack. He gave the Hammertail a scratch around the ear. "Don't wander off. I'm going to need you."

Daniel turned back, took a running jump, and—

Whompff!!!

Daniel's Aegis burst into action, creating a controlled wave of iridescent energy that propelled him up and into the opening ripped into the side of the *Coldstar.*

He'd gotten good at controlling this thing.

Daniel landed on one knee and scrutinized his surroundings.

The metal hexagons on his Truth Seeker uniform glinted in the dim light.

A short maintenance passage of some type stretched out before him. The buckled floor had weeds growing up through the grilles. At one time this floor had been the ceiling, but with the ship on its back everything was upside down. Pipes lined either side of the passageway leading down to a heavy pressure door where Jasper was already tinkering with the mechanism to get it to open.

"Stand back," Daniel ordered.

Jasper shook his flippers, trying to indicate that he almost had it, but Daniel didn't feel like waiting. The anatom searched for cover while Daniel reached out his hand. His Aegis swirled, generating a power blast that crushed the lock. The door shook and creaked before sliding open.

Daniel activated his own F-light and tossed it into the

area beyond. He didn't really know what to expect . . .

. . . but this wasn't it: An opulent-looking hallway, wide and deep, ran perpendicular to the maintenance passage. Thick carpet lined the ceiling. It had rotted now, and hung down in sheets like the creepers outside. It must have looked magnificent back in the day when it used to be the floor. Ornate golden patterns lined the walls, and pictures hung at steady intervals along an endless line of doorways, each one marked with a number.

"What kind of ship is this?" Daniel wondered. It reminded him of the hotel in Loronoh, Oota Mheen's capital city, where the Truth Seekers had set up a temporary headquarters for the impending invasion. "This isn't a military vessel," he said. "This is a passenger ship."

Other than the name *Coldstar*, what was his connection to this starliner? The questions multiplied. Why had it crashed? Why did somebody want him to come here and see it? Who was that somebody?

Daniel beckoned to Jasper to keep up. "Come on. We need to find the bridge," he said, leaping down onto what had once been the ceiling.

Jasper waddled along the vertical wall as though it were the most normal thing in the world to do, humming an oddly cheerful little song.

"We're looking for the databanks," Daniel explained, assuming that that was what the penguin wanted to know. "If they're intact, they're my best hope of finding some answers. Think you can copy the data from them?"

Jasper made a rude grunting noise and shook his head.

"Well, why not?"

The anatom ceased his hum and switched to some tuneless funeral dirge.

"Can we at least retrieve them?"

Jasper shrugged. *Maybe.*

Daniel glanced around, trying to get a sense of the layout. "Any idea where the bridge is from here?"

Jasper looked for an answer, zeroing in on a data port halfway up the wall. His yellow light-wire crest glowed briefly as each feather extended out into the receptacle, probing for a connection. A moment later the light-wire feathers pulsed brightly as the data transfer began, faster and faster until—

Sssnappp!

An arc of electricity zipped out of the port, showering the anatom in a cascade of sparks.

Jasper lost his grip and fell to the ground with a heavy *thud!*

Daniel held out his hands. "Well? Where do we go?"

The flustered penguin shook his head before jabbing a flipper into the air.

They needed to go up.

Which of course meant down if the *Coldstar* had been right side up. It seemed that this class of starliner mounted its command center on the very lowest point of the vessel.

Clink! Clink! Clink! Clink! Clink!

"Hold it!" Daniel warned, listening to what sounded like distant footsteps scurrying around the abandoned wreck not far from where they stood. Animals? People? Hard to say.

"Let's go," Daniel urged quietly, helping Jasper up. "Keep your eyes open. I don't think we're alone in here."

They climbed up through twenty or so mangled decks, before Daniel's utility belt chirped. Someone was trying to call. Reluctantly, he ran his palm through the air, bringing up the holographic display. The call was coming from the Seventh Summit, his home with the Truth Seekers on Orpheus Core.

Nails's image popped up, floating in front of him. As long as he lived, Daniel was pretty sure he would never get used to seeing someone with fingernails for hair.

"I told you not to contact me unless it's an emergency. Anyone could be listening in," Daniel said.

Henegan Rann's face briefly crowded into the picture. Rann, Nails, and Fix Suncharge; they were the only other grubs who had made it out of the relic mines when Daniel and the Truth Seekers had come to rescue them.

"This *is* an emergency," Rann said.

Nails pushed him away. "Do you mind?"

"What's going on?" demanded Daniel.

"Time's up," said Nails.

"The Tarafand invasion force is here?" Daniel quipped.

He knew they were still days away.

"Worse."

"Worse? How can it be worse?"

"They're looking for you."

"*Who* are looking for me?"

"Ionica. Ben. They know you're missing. They're out combing the entire area, searching for you."

Daniel dismissed the news by shifting the image to one side so he could still see where he was going. "We knew that would happen." He glanced down at Jasper. The anatom led the way, gesturing for him to follow. Not far now.

"Disappearing in the middle of a rescue mission to go off on this little adventure was never a good idea," Nails insisted.

"What other chance was I going to get?" Daniel argued. It would have been easy to have listened to them back at the Seventh Summit and forgotten about this whole risky venture, but that wasn't who Daniel was. If it had been, he never would have escaped the relic mines in the first place.

"Well, guess what?" Daniel said. "I found it."

Surprise drifted across Nails's face like a sun sliding out from behind a cloud. "Are you serious? It's *real*?"

"Yes, it's real. It's right where he said it would be—"

"*Who* said it would be there?" An angry voice cut in.

Everyone froze.

Busted.

Nobody knew what to say at first. How long had Ionica

Lux been eavesdropping on this channel?

Nails gulped. "I think she can hear us."

"You *think*?" said Daniel.

"Hey, Nails," Ionica said, changing her tone. "Did you get your nails done?"

Completely disarmed, Nails ran a hand over his recent headicure. What used to look like shriveled, bumpy brown scales had transformed into smooth and thick nails through good nutrition and proper care. Now they were painted in iridescent colors, with a sleek pink stripe along one side, stretching from front to back.

"Yes," he said. "Do you like it?"

"Like it? I love it!"

"Thanks," Nails replied bashfully.

"I tell you what. If you don't want me to pull your nails out one at a time, get off this channel."

Daniel rolled his eyes, but Nails took the intimidation seriously. He grimaced and ended the call.

"Daniel Coldstar, where are you?" Ionica demanded.

Daniel and Jasper had reached the doors to the bridge. After a little anatomic tinkering they flew open and the pair stepped into what had once been the functioning command center of the starliner.

Above them, the upside-down seating and consoles were arranged on a ring-shaped deck with an enormous clear bubble of carbonic glass beyond that, which would have been the floor once upon a time. Daniel suspected the idea was to give the crew a clear view of the docking platforms whenever the ship arrived at its destinations on a cruise. Now the glass bubble served as a roof, covered in vines, nests, and animal droppings.

"Are you going to answer me?" Ionica said.

"What does it matter?"

"It matters because war is about to explode across this entire planet! When the Tarafand arrive, *nowhere* will be safe. We'll have to evacuate."

"I don't understand why the Sinja don't just fight their own battles," Daniel replied. "They do have the Mythrian Army now."

"Have you seen any sign of that army, anywhere in the galaxy, in the past year?"

"Nope." He jabbed a finger at what appeared to be the ship's databanks, a large array of computer equipment that sat around the rim of the room. "See what you can retrieve," he whispered to Jasper.

"I heard that!"

Jasper shrugged and went to work, producing a screwdriver from a compartment at the end of his flipper.

"You know how the Sinja operate, Daniel," Ionica added. "Why fight a war when you can get two planets to destroy each other *for* you? That's what they've been doing ever since they got their hands on the Book of Planets."

"Don't you think I know that?" Daniel snapped angrily. "The whole galaxy is in chaos because of *me*. This planet is now at war with the Tarafand *because of me*."

It had been an elaborate scheme to be sure, but nobody could deny that the many star nations spread across the galaxy would not be in this position if it had not been for Daniel leading his supposed ally Hex, an anatom compromised by the Sinja, right to the Book of Planets in the Truth Seeker Vault.

An ancient relic with incredible power, the Book of Planets revealed all, from the weather to the complete defenses of every planet in the galaxy. Since Hex had stolen it and delivered it to the Sinja, the galaxy had descended into turmoil. The Sinja had fomented war on countless worlds by supplying opposing alliances with information obtained from that very book. Mixing in truth with just enough lies and suspicion to create panic. Refugees streamed across the galaxy trying to escape the chaos that reigned supreme.

"Daniel," Ionica replied quietly, "that's not what I meant."

Daniel didn't want to hear it. "Look," he said. "I won't be much longer, and I'll be back to help."

"Why should I believe you?" she insisted.

"Because I said so!"

A loud *slammmm!*

Daniel froze. Jasper stopped what he was doing and looked up.

Something had just landed on the dome and was tearing at the hull to get inside. To get to *them.*

"Just trust me," Daniel whispered. "But now I have to go."

3
SHOWDOWN

The deafening sound of ruptured metal filled the destroyed command center.

Carbonic glass looked like ordinary glass, but it acted like metal and did not shatter. Instead, a slice of the dome peeled back like the skin on fruit, raining dirt and debris down into the room.

A moment later, Daniel heard the visitor land on the underside of the command ring with a thud. The visitor paced back and forth, searching.

Daniel bided his time. Waited for his moment. When the visitor jumped down right behind him—Daniel did not flinch.

The visitor reached out. Grabbed him. Turned him around. Only to have Daniel smile and evaporate in a cloud of holocule dust. The programmable matter-energy molecules, more solid and real than a hologram, served as the perfect decoy.

Confused, the visitor whirled around, only to find herself thrust into the light as the real Daniel emerged from the shadows and pinned her to a buckled support column.

"Ionica?"

Ionica Lux seemed different somehow. In the shadows, her pale skin virtually glowed, while her long dark hair, tied in a ponytail and secured with Hemma beads, seemed to melt into the darkness.

She blinked at him. "Sinja tactics. Really?"

"What? No! Just tactics," Daniel protested. "How did you find me?"

"I'm surprised the whole galaxy didn't find you," she said. Then she too burst into a cloud of holocule dust.

Another perfect decoy.

"Hey, not fair!" He spun around in frustration. Where was she? How did she find him—? Wait a second. He snapped his fingers. "You followed Alice's trail through the jungle? Am I right?"

"No," Ionica called back. "Though if you'd just learn to skyride there wouldn't be a trail through the jungle to follow. You could have jumped here."

Daniel zeroed in on her voice. She was still outside. "Sure," he said. "And jump in blind? You know they call this place the Death Jungles for a reason."

He stepped out from under the dusty command ring to see Ionica standing in the sunlight on the edge of the hole she'd created, hands on her hips. Her uniform gleamed in the light.

Daniel rolled his eyes. "Can't you ever just use a door? Seriously, how did you find me?"

"The same way anyone can find you. That signal from your Identifier is readable from a hundred miles away."

Daniel exhaled slowly. His Identifier. Most days he tried not to think about the blasted thing, but it loomed over his life like a bad smell. In the relic mines, the Sinja had implanted a socket into each grub's head to control them. Identifiers were tiny chips inserted into a socket's control circuits that told an Overseer who they were dealing with so they didn't have to think. With thousands of grubs to deal with, Overseers hated having to think.

"We've gone over this a million times," said Ionica. "Quit wandering off on your own. Remember that headhunter back on Safatee? You're a walking target. The Sinja want you dead. If I can find you, they can."

"I can defend myself," Daniel said. "Besides, that chip'll be gone soon. Astrid's got it all figured out." He turned his back on her to help Jasper remove the panels from the databanks.

Ionica had clearly never heard such garbage. "No she doesn't."

Daniel ignored her.

"What are you doing?"

"Removing the data panel. What does it look like I'm doing?"

Ionica grimaced. "You'll never get it open if you do it like that."

Daniel gritted his teeth, twisting the release pins around and around. "I've got this. They're coming loose."

"No they're not."

"They *are*! I can feel it."

"You have to push them in. Use your thumbs."

"I know what I'm doing!"

Out of patience, Ionica jumped down into the room for real this time and elbowed Daniel out of the way. She pressed the release pins with her thumbs. The panel fell away.

"You're annoying," said Daniel.

Jasper gave an approving hum.

"So, is the ship named after you," she asked, "or are you named after the ship?"

"That's what I'm trying to figure out," Daniel replied.

"Well, whatever the answer, we *have* to go. The Tarafand are here—"

"Wait a minute, what do you mean, they're *here*? They can't be here. Guardian Alioth said they were days away."

"This is a *war zone*. Things change. Now we have our orders to collect the refugees and get out of here. We can't get caught in the middle of this. Come on."

"I can't leave," Daniel insisted. "Not until I get what I came here for." Reaching around inside the databank, he fumbled until he found a release mechanism and carefully slid a data core out of its housing. The cube-shaped object, a solid crystal wrapped in a latticed metal jacket, weighed far more than its appearance would suggest.

He dropped the cube into his backpack and moved on to the next computer bank.

"Daniel," Ionica insisted. "You're a Truth Seeker. You have a responsibility to the people trying to flee Oota Mheen."

"Then maybe I shouldn't be a Truth Seeker anymore," Daniel snapped, poking around for more cores.

"What's that supposed to mean?"

Daniel ignored the question. "Just let me finish up and we can get out of here." He eased another data core out of its housing. "You okay over there, Jasper?"

The anatomic penguin hummed cheerfully as it dragged two data cores over to Daniel's backpack and deposited them inside—

Chirp, chirp . . . Chirp, chirp . . .

The communications bleep came from Ionica's utility belt.

Daniel gave her an uneasy look. "The *Equinox*?"

She nodded, opening the channel to the mighty splintership.

Daniel couldn't see Ionica's holographic screen from his

angle, and she had the comms audio fed directly into her ear, but he got the gist when he heard her say: "I found him. He's okay. Little Daniel got lost."

When she ended the conversation, Daniel said, "Hey, I'm not lost! I know exactly where I am."

"Please. I was just protecting you."

"I don't need you to protect me."

"Of course you do," she said. "*You're* not going to do it. Now, are you done?"

Daniel nodded, slinging the heavy pack over his back. "How much time do we have?"

"Twenty minutes," Ionica said. "Or they leave without us." She glanced around at what was left of the ship. "How did you even find this place?" she asked.

But Daniel did not have a chance to reply. All around them, the shadows were moving.

In the blink of an eye, the two Truth Seekers ignited their Aegis shields, defensively standing back-to-back, bracing themselves for what was to come.

But neither of them was prepared for what emerged.

4

THE HIDDEN

A small figure edged nervously toward them; it was a child, frail and hungry.

He was perhaps five or six years old. His shaved head and torn clothes were filthy. In a voice as quiet as the night, he asked, "Did Ammee send you?"

Daniel and Ionica eyed each other and lowered their shields. What was this kid doing here?

"Who might you be?" Ionica asked gently, kneeling down, trying to put the boy at ease.

He retreated a step, unsure how he was supposed to react.

"Who is Ammee?" Daniel asked. This kid looked too familiar. Too much like everyone he remembered back in the mines. Too much like his failure to rescue them and the nightmares that had come since that failure.

"Ammee," the boy replied. "Ammee and Baba." Maybe they were local words, some Oota Mheen slang, or maybe they were just words the boy had made up. Either way, the sheer longing in his eyes told them everything they needed to know.

"Mommy and Daddy?" Ionica asked.

The boy nodded.

"I'm Ionica," she said. "This is Daniel. What's your name?"

The boy glanced back toward the other shadows, uncertain of whether he needed their permission.

"Are they your friends? They can come out now. It's okay."

The boy shook his head. The shadows stayed where they were.

"Where did your ammee go?" Ionica asked gently.

"To the war," he said simply.

"How long have you been here?"

The boy shrugged. "Ammee said it would be safe. She said no one would look for us here."

"Safe?" Daniel replied, perplexed. "This place?" There couldn't be a more dangerous place on this entire planet. "How long have you been here?"

The boy shrugged again. "I don't know."

"Tillowil!" a small voice cried from the shadows. A girl's voice. "Tillowil, I'm hungry."

Annoyed, the boy turned to the shadows, raising a finger to his lips. "Shh! Kember!"

Ionica rose to her feet, peering into the darkness with him. "We have food," she said quickly. "Here." She reached into her utility belt and pulled out an emergency ration. "It's not much, but you can have it."

Daniel followed her lead, pulling out a handful of the tiny energy-packed bars. "Take mine too," he said. "You'd be doing me a favor, actually."

Tillowil's eyes lit up as though he'd just discovered the greatest treasure in all the galaxy.

"We can get more. If you come with us, I'm sure we can feed *all* of you," Ionica insisted.

"How many of you are there?" asked Daniel, tossing an emergency ration into the dark. He heard the scuffle of feet as the other children fought over the food. He guessed maybe ten or fifteen.

He guessed wrong.

Slowly, very slowly, the children of the shadows shuffled into the light, revealing face after starving face. Their eyes sunken, their cheeks stretched thin. Each child wore a mask of horror.

There were perhaps as many as a hundred. And all it took to gain their trust was the promise of food.

Something wasn't right here. Daniel felt it in the pit of his stomach. He'd played this game before with the Overseers and the Sinja. Anything could have crept into the wreck of the *Coldstar* and attacked these kids. Why hadn't it? Because this was how they broke them. Their child soldiers. They took them. They abandoned them. Left them in danger.

And then with the promise of help—they "saved" them.

"We have to get them out of here," Daniel said.

"All of them?" Ionica scoffed, still reeling from the sheer numbers of children who were crowding around.

"We're not leaving them," Daniel insisted.

"Of course not! But how do we get them through the jungle alive?"

"We'll figure it out!"

They would have to figure it out quickly.

The *Coldstar* shuddered and groaned, and the air filled with the rage of engines as warships streaked across the skies above them.

5

DARK SKIES

"Ben, we need a miracle," Daniel said.

"This whole bloody planet needs a miracle," Ben Quick replied, on edge. The two boys could see for a hundred miles across the treetops. Crouched on the edge of the ruptured dome, they watched as a deafening swarm of Tarafand forces flew low over the jungle—fighters, bombers, troop landers—all headed for their target over the horizon: Loronoh, the capital city.

Ben shimmered briefly, losing form, before fusing back together. Another holocule projection, but with good reason. Seeing through the eyes of a holocule avatar was as good as Ben actually being there, and made it easier for him to get an idea of Daniel's situation. Physically, Ben was still aboard the *Equinox*.

He reminded Daniel of Blink a little, with those same Burn World eyes with no pupils. Though his personality was completely different; cocky, sometimes overconfident. His hair was always scruffy, his boots never fastened properly.

A look of panic washed over him. "The first wave has arrived—" Ben ducked to the sound of an explosion Daniel couldn't see. "Crikey, that was close!"

Daniel winced. "Stay safe, will you?"

"That's rich, coming from you. Didn't you just ask me to fly a cargo pod through an invasion force to come pick you up?"

Actually it was worse than that. These transports didn't have any weapons or defensive capabilities of any kind. Though Daniel wasn't about to remind his old roommate of that.

"Can't you pilot it remotely?"

Ben scoffed. "Where's the fun in that—?" His eyes widened. "Oh, blimey . . ."

Ben's holocule image shattered for good this time, followed by an enormous flash of light erupting over the horizon.

Panicked, Daniel opened a channel. "Ben! Can you hear me? Ben?!"

Nothing.

He snatched his trinoculars up from his belt. They were an old set, but they did the job. Three sensor rods automatically eased out, triangulating on each target to give super-accurate distance readings.

Exactly 123 miles and 18.4 paces away, he watched the war erupt over the capital city. Oota Mheenish lava cannons opened fire on approaching craft. Superheated rock dust flashed through the air, looking like energy weapon bursts except that when these blasts made contact they stuck like glue and burned through their targets.

Shoom! Shoom! Shoom!

Defensive fighters raced to engage the Tarafand amid a cloud of—was that a flock of birds?

Daniel zoomed in.

No. Tiny flashes sparked down their backs. These were Thunderheads—airborne troops wearing rocket packs.

Daniel felt the blood drain from his face. "Oh no." He tried the channel again. "Ben? Can you hear me? Ben, come in."

No answer.

"I lost Ben!" Daniel yelled back down to Ionica, who was still rounding the kids up for the evacuation. Seeing them all, Daniel wondered if a single cargo pod was going to be enough.

"Try someone else!" Ionica hollered back.

"I'm worried about Ben!"

"Worry about *them*!" she shot back, gesturing at the kids.

He glanced down into the ship. Nearly a hundred sets of tiny eyes peered back at him. The frightened children said nothing, but then they didn't need to.

Daniel hesitated, but he had no choice. He had to activate the emergency channel. Even if he was going to get an earful from Guardian Raze Alioth when he found out what was going on.

Oh well. It was going to happen sooner or later anyway.

He hammered the emergency channel. "This is Beacon Daniel Coldstar to anyone who can hear us—we need immediate evacuation. I repeat, immediate evacuation. Beacon Lux and I have found about a hundred refugees. All children—"

Overhead, a Tarafand troopship suddenly changed direction, circling back toward the wreck of the *Coldstar*.

It had picked up his signal.

Hatches in the ship's gleaming underbelly snapped open and Thunderheads started pouring out, boosters ablaze. They landed in the forest, not too far off.

The bottom fell out of Daniel's stomach. How the heck were he and Ionica, a couple of apprentice Truth Seekers, supposed to take on an entire squad of well-armed, stone-cold, battle-hardened Thunderheads?

His voice warbled. "There are enemy troops on the ground! I repeat, Tarafand troops are heading this way!"

A tone squealed down the channel, followed by a gruff voice. "This is Guardian Alioth. We have received your distress call and have your position. We'll talk about why you're out there later."

Busted.

"Yes, sir," Daniel replied, trying to keep his voice flat. "I understand."

"Good, because I don't. Truth Seekers, I need a volunteer—"

"Already on it," a voice cut in from out of nowhere. "On final approach now."

"Ben! You're okay!" Daniel cried.

"Of course I'm okay."

Relieved, Daniel craned his neck, trying to figure out which direction Ben was coming from. *There!* To the south, gliding out from behind a line of jagged foothills, a bulky cargo pod approaching at the speed of a glacier.

"All Truth Seekers," Alioth continued, sounding grim, "the Sinja have masterfully infected these two societies with so many falsehoods that the people can no longer distinguish truth from fiction. Sinja influence has convinced both sides that *we* are the enemy. It is therefore no longer viable for us to remain. We knew this would be a risk, but we had to try.

"We are now commencing a total evacuation of all Truth Seekers from this planet. Anyone not aboard their vessels within the hour will be left behind. The refugees are our priority. Godspeed, everyone."

A knot tightened in Daniel's stomach. This was his fault. This was *all* his fault. The moment he let the Book of Planets fall into the hands of the Sinja, he had betrayed the entire galaxy, and there was nothing he could do about it now.

THRUMMMMMMMM!

The cumbersome cargo pod hovered above the wreck, its load thrusters growling. Slowly, it eased down onto the rusting hull, massive load-bearing landing gear splaying out like feet.

With a *hiss* the back end popped open, a grimy loading ramp eased out, and Ben barreled outside. "Come on, we haven't got all day! Where are they?"

Whompff!

Ionica directed an Aegis blast at the ground and flew up out of the dome with two of the smaller kids, one under each arm. They landed softly at the foot of the ramp. "Do we have any rope?"

Ben raced to the grubby loading controls mounted on the bulkhead by the entrance. "I know what we can use."

Ka-chunk! Ka-chunk! Ka-chunk!

Greasy hatches sprang open down the center of the cargo pod's loading deck, revealing spooled cargo nets. Daniel grabbed one by its pair of tritanium hooks and jumped back down into the bridge, unraveling the net as he went.

"Watch your toesies!" Ionica urged, jumping down with him. The kids scattered.

Daniel handed her one of the hooks. "Here," he said. "Do something useful."

Ionica narrowed her eyes. "*Me* do something useful?"

"Uh, guys?" Ben called out. "I see soldiers. They're carrying blasers. Hurry it up."

Blasers: handheld lava cannons. One good shot and the molten bullet would eat through anything.

Daniel scratched about for whatever he could find. The grille over that air duct might work. He secured his end of the netting to that, while Ionica raced to the other side of the bridge and did the same thing, opening the full expanse out to create a makeshift ladder.

"Go!"

The children surged forward, scrambling up the netting, wiping away tears with filthy hands.

Fzzt! Fzzt! Fzzt!

Sizzling blaser fire ripped over their heads, burning the very air they breathed.

"Go help Ben!" Daniel insisted. "I'll make sure they get up there."

Ionica nodded, taking two more of the smaller kids with her. "Hold on tight," she said, before zipping up into the air with a *whompff!*

Daniel directed the next wave of terrified children to get climbing. As they scrambled over the lip of the breach and clambered onto the outside of the ship, an alarm blared from deep inside the cargo pod: *"Warning! Load capacity exceeded. Warning! Load capacity exceeded."*

"Ben!" Daniel yelled. "What does that mean?"

"Hold on!" Ben hollered back.

"We still have kids down here!"

"I know! Give me a minute!"

"We don't have a minute!"

Daniel clenched his teeth, trying to keep his cool. It didn't help that this Tillowil kid and the last remaining handful of refugees were watching him while he pretended to hold it together. "It'll be okay," he said.

They didn't look like they believed him.

Ionica peered down from the edge of the rupture overhead. She looked shaken. "We can't take any more," she said quietly. "Or the pod won't fly."

Daniel didn't have to look at the children to know that tears had started to spill down their cheeks. He lifted his chin. "We're not leaving them here," he said.

"We'll come back," she promised.

"There's no time."

"Daniel," she pleaded. "We'll figure something out."

A hum, low and soothing, drifted over from the far corner of the bridge. Jasper! In all the activity Daniel had forgotten all about the little anatom, still standing there clutching a backpack full of data cores.

The penguin made a farting noise and waved a flipper in front of his beak.

Of course! Maybe there *was* a way out of this after all.

"Go," Daniel said, shooing Ionica away. "Go. I'll get them out with Alice."

"That's too dangerous with all the Thunderheads around," she said.

"It's better than being a sitting target," Daniel replied.

The remaining children watched, helpless, as Ionica cut the netting loose. It fell to the ground with a thud.

They listened to the whine of lifting thrusters shifting into high power and watched as the cargo pod flew away.

"This isn't over," Daniel said. "Come on. Follow me."

6

THE LORONOH RUN

Daniel improvised in a hurry.

Alice had a Turan howdah, a combo riding and pack-saddle, strapped to his broad back. Daniel dumped the supplies—they wouldn't need them anyway if they were dead—but he kept the saddlebags. Two of the smaller kids could ride in those. That left figuring out how to get the other five onto a trabasaur and keep them there for the duration of their escape run.

Daniel watched the jungle. Everything looked the same. Sounded the same. Stank the same. No sign of those Tarafand soldiers. Not yet, anyway. So why was his skin crawling?

One by one, the kids emerged from the hole in the side of the *Coldstar* and scampered down the creepers anchored to its hull. They each hit the ground running and raced over to Daniel, ready to help.

"What about this?" Tillowil suggested, dragging a filthy sheet of tough orange fabric behind him. He dumped it out in the open.

Judging from the markings, this thing used to be part of an emergency shelter.

Daniel yanked at both ends in an attempt to get it to rip. It held solid. "Yes," he said quickly. "Everyone see what we can use for fastenings."

The kids scattered their finds on the ground and set to work while Daniel relieved Jasper of his very full backpack.

The anatom dragged the orange sheeting toward Alice.

"You think you can make this work?" Daniel asked.

Jasper did not respond, instead concentrating on cutting the tough fabric into strips and fashioning them into continuous loops. When the first one was ready, the anatom held it out, gesturing for Daniel to toss it over Alice's packsaddle and fasten it in the center. It was only when that was done that Daniel realized what Jasper had created. A loop of fabric now hung on either side of Alice, creating slings that the children could ride in.

After a few more precious minutes, the other slings were ready and it was time to load up.

Alice gave the first kid a curious glance, trying to figure out if he should trust him or not.

Daniel fastened scavenged cables to the center of the

packsaddle and quickly began tying them around the kids' waists. "This is going to get bumpy," he warned.

He threw himself into the saddle and grabbed Alice's reins. "Hang on!" he cried, and with the tap of his feet and a hearty *"Yah!"* he got the beast running.

They charged into the jungle, bounding over fallen trunks and galloping through brackish water.

"Faster!" Daniel urged, digging his heels in.

Alice put his head down and lengthened his stride. The ground shook. The children hung on, bouncing around, ducking for cover every time a bough of black vegetation swiped at them.

Daniel crouched lower, using every muscle he had to not get thrown right out of the saddle. Ahead, a clump of tangled trees blocked their way. In a flash, Daniel activated his Aegis—

Whompff!

A skillfully controlled wall of air crackled with electricity and rose up around the Hammertail, ripping leaves and twigs from their branches and hammering into the clump of trees in front of them. The trunks split and tore and were flung behind them with an almighty *thwack!*

Plowing through, Alice barreled headlong into a gigantic trap-bloom. The massive leaves curled up instantly, sinking dagger-sized thorns into his hind leg. A long pink tendril shot up from its throat, wrapping itself around Alice's thigh like a serpent's tongue.

41

The children screamed and kicked, but Alice was in no mood to be eaten today.

The Hammertail ran, and with every ounce of his considerable strength, ripped the trap-bloom from the dirt, dragging its fleshy bag-like body along behind. The plant made a dreadful yelping sound when something pierced its translucent flesh, and out spilled stomach acid and undigested bits of unlucky forest dwellers.

Without breaking stride, Alice flicked his leg, tossing the trap-bloom into the air, and whacked it with his spiky tail, shredding it to pieces.

Daniel glanced back over his shoulder with a triumphant grimace, patting Alice on the back of the neck.

When he turned back around, he realized that their situation had not improved.

Shmm-Pew! Shmm-Pew! Shmm-Pew!

Angry red blaser fire exploded out of the dense jungle foliage from every direction. Trees and creepers burst into flames, their burning leaves leaping into the air like demonic fireflies.

The Tarafand had found them.

7

JARANJARS!

Daniel tugged on the reins.

Alice bucked to a stop, padding left and right, trying to figure out a way through, but there was nowhere to go.

Tarafand Thunderheads, with their armored uniforms as dark as the jungle around them, crept from their hiding spots, blocking every exit they hadn't set ablaze.

One of the soldiers, with the red marking of a commander on his shoulder, raised a fist, ordering the squad to cease fire.

"You're a Truth Seeker," the commander remarked.

It was hard to know what the soldiers intended, since their faces were hidden behind helmets. Just in case they harbored any doubts about their star nation's decision to turn on the Guild of Truth, Daniel dug deep for some courage.

"Yes, I'm a Truth Seeker," he said. "So you'll let us pass if you know what's good for you." His hands shook. They had to know he was bluffing.

The Tarafand commander took another ominous step toward him, not intimidated in the slightest. "Where are you taking those children?"

They knew. Bluff called. Change the subject.

"What are you doing on this planet?" Daniel fired back.

"Those do not belong to you," the commander persisted.

Those? It sounded like he was talking about things, not people. "These *children* don't *belong to* anyone," Daniel said with disgust, his mouth dry. "They belong *with* their parents."

"They have no parents," came the grim response.

Everything about that statement revolted Daniel. "That's a lie," he said.

"Where are the others?" the commander demanded.

"What others?" Daniel said quickly, feigning ignorance. Why would an invading army know about a bunch of kids stashed away in the middle of nowhere? This wasn't adding up.

The Tarafand commander signaled one of his underlings. "Inform Vega Virrus that our gift to him has been compromised. Assure him that we will be sending our apology and to expect the head of a Truth Seeker instead."

So now they weren't even trying to hide their allegiance to the Sinja.

Daniel flung up an Aegis shield as fast as he could, prompting Alice to roar angrily.

The Thunderheads opened fire, each glowing lava blast hitting the whirling vortex with a *blam* before rebounding off at an angle.

Alice backed away, trying not to get his tail caught in the flames.

There had to be a way out of this, there had to be!

With the terrified kids screaming all around him, Daniel searched desperately for an escape route, but there wasn't one. Even Jasper seemed to be out of ideas—when suddenly the firing stopped! In complete disarray, the Thunderheads ran around shrieking at each other. The soldiers turned their attention to the leafy canopy and to the hanging vines that were silently wrapping themselves around their throats and dragging them up into the trees one by one.

Roaaar-khu-kha . . . ! Roaaar-kha-kha . . . !

The Tarafand commander fired blindly into the treetops, setting branch after branch ablaze until—

Thud!

A massive Jaranjar dropped down from the branches. Standing on two legs, it towered over the commander and was perhaps two or three times his size. Its face was like a big cat's. Its tail, muscular and stretching for several body lengths, curled and quivered. Its apelike body shimmered with silver stripes sparkling like comets over its black velvet coat. It opened its mouth, and with huge serrated teeth gleaming white—it roared.

Alice raged at the creature.

The Jaranjar raged back, only to howl in agony as the fur across its back exploded in flames. The furious animal swung around, lashing out at the Tarafand commander, using its powerful tail to grab him and smash him into a tree trunk.

"Now's our chance!" Daniel cried, spurring Alice on. *"Yah!"*

The Hammertail launched into a gallop, leaving the battle far, far behind.

They plowed blindly through thick foliage for mile after mile without any thought to what was waiting for them, until the jungle began to thin. The skies overhead filled with starfighters. Streaks of energy and flashes of light burst between the clouds. Engines flamed out. Ships tumbled.

None of it made a difference to Daniel, who urged Alice onward, never letting up, never letting him slow. An old track opened up a little farther on, leading to the jagged ruins of a bombed-out town. Shredded flags and propaganda urging all Oota Mheenish citizens to join the glorious war against the Tarafand hung limply in the rubble, omitting the fact that they weren't exactly good guys either.

"*Equinox*? Come in, *Equinox*!" Daniel pleaded over an open channel, desperately checking his map.

Thirty miles? They'd only gone *thirty miles*? They were

never going to make it in time!

"Equinox!"

Why wasn't anybody answering? Had they left already?

"Equinox, please . . . ," Daniel begged, his voice broken.

Ninety-three more miles? How in all the galaxy were they going to run ninety-three miles in the next ten minutes—

FFFFRRRRROOOOOOMMMMMMMMM!

Every molecule in the air shook as though the very atmosphere around them wanted to rip apart.

A shadow, massive and dark, slid over Daniel and the children.

The roar of mighty engines grew deafening. Daniel's ears began to ache.

And then—

A ship descended right in front of them. Like a giant silver starfish, cargo pods retrofitted to the ends of her long arms instead of her usual complement of Spitfires. The scars of galactic strife etched into her skin.

The *Equinox* had come for them.

8

THE REFUGEES

"Mr. Coldstar," *Truth Guardian* Alioth ordered, gesturing with his finger. "Come here."

Daniel gulped. He really didn't want to go over there. Taking one reluctant step after another, he forced himself to do as he was told.

All around the Sphere, the *Equinox*'s impressive command center, ships and blasts crisscrossed through the REPIS view and targeting system. One by one, each ship in the humanitarian convoy jumped to Inspinity, while Truth Seekers who sat at stations on the upper level of the Sphere piloted drones and held the Oota Mheenish and Tarafand forces at bay.

A young Truth Seeker glanced up from her station. "They made it, sir," she said. "All ships have been evacuated."

Alioth seemed satisfied. "Good. Now thread the needle and get us out of here."

Daniel watched the stars streak and tumble as the *Equinox* entered light speed.

"Message ahead to Orpheus Core," Alioth added. "Mark Oota Mheen off-limits to all Truth Seekers. Let it be known these two star nations are now free to continue their bid to annihilate one another unencumbered by the truth or any sense of humanity."

The young Truth Seeker, her face ashen, nodded when she had sent the message.

"You wanted to see me, sir?" Daniel asked quietly.

Truth Guardian Alioth was intimidating enough with his broad shoulders and the peculiar humidifier under his nose, expelling gases that the people of his world had evolved to rely upon. But he was not alone this time. Other Truth Seekers and Guardians stood with him. They had been huddled for some time in heated discussion over the events on Oota Mheen, the state of the galaxy, and what the Guild of Truth's next move should be.

"You're a very lucky young man, aren't you, Mr. Coldstar?" Alioth remarked in a tone that might have been related to humor. It was difficult to tell.

"I don't feel lucky," Daniel replied. What he felt was their eyes all burning into him. What else was he supposed to say?

"Really, Mr. Coldstar?" said Alioth. "You just happened

to get lost in one of the most dangerous forests in this part of the galaxy, and you just *happened* to find refugees, children no less, who were facing an impending life of misery under the Sinja, not unlike the one you yourself once lived? I don't believe in coincidences. Do you, Mr. Coldstar?"

How was he going to answer this one? "No, sir" just didn't seem adequate.

"I wasn't lost," Daniel corrected. At least that was the truth.

It was clear from their faces that no one had been expecting that response.

"I went to see that ship," he explained.

"Why?" one of the others asked.

Daniel recognized her instantly. Master Skyrider Hella Phad, with hair like fire, and her fists on her hips. He'd seen her dart in and out of the clouds like a lightning bolt over the Fortress of Truth many times.

Daniel had never seen Ionica so excited to take classes with anyone before. Ionica was the first skyrider he'd ever known. She knew how to control her Aegis and fly better than anyone. Daniel could leap and bounce around, but he couldn't do *that*. When he'd first met Ionica, she'd boarded the ship he was on without a space suit but with a bubble of air inside a force field. So for Ionica to be in such awe of Hella Phad spoke volumes.

Daniel considered his answer carefully. "I heard a rumor—someone told me about it."

"Who?" she asked.

"I don't know their name," he answered.

Alioth folded his arms. "Why would somebody just decide to tell you about a crashed ship in the middle of nowhere? And why would they think you would be interested?"

"Because it has my name on it. It's called the *Coldstar*," Daniel admitted, aware that although nothing he had said was a lie, it also wasn't the whole story. "I just wanted to see if I had any connection to it. I thought maybe it could help me find out who I really am," he added desperately.

He braced himself for an angry response, but Guardian Alioth just nodded. "I understand," he said. "I may have done the same thing if I were in your position."

Daniel felt the tension melt from his shoulders.

"However," Alioth added forcefully, "your actions put lives at risk. Your friend Ionica, your friend Ben. Every Truth Seeker who went out looking for you was put at risk! Every refugee looking to us for protection was put at risk because we were distracted! Searching *for you*. Do you understand?"

Daniel gazed down at his feet, shame washing over him. "I'm sorry," he said, his voice barely audible.

"The only thing saving you from an official reprimand and being held back a year are these refugees you uncovered," Alioth explained. "And *that*, Mr. Coldstar, is why you are very lucky. Do you understand?"

Daniel nodded. "Yes, sir, I understand."

"These children are now your responsibility," he added. "Camp Five informs me they have room. You will arrange their accommodations, clean clothes, food, and water. You will get them entered into the logs so they can begin looking for their families. Are there any questions?"

Daniel shook his head. "No, sir."

The *Equinox* burst out of Inspinity at Orpheus Core, a little farther out than normal. Any closer and there was a serious risk of a collision.

In recent months, so many refugee ships from so many worlds had moved into orbit around the Truth Seeker base that the War Guild had stationed ships nearby to protect them. Ships of all shapes and sizes crowded the skies over Orpheus Core. There were passenger ships, converted freighters, and caravan haulers.

Across the planet's surface, evacuation camps now sprawled like tented cities radiating out for mile upon mile, filled with millions of families who had lost everything.

It was a cruel galaxy, and these camps were only a temporary break from it. The refugees would be moving on in time, following the promise of permanent new homes. Yet as one family left, three more arrived to replace them, and the camps continued to grow.

Swooping over the Fortress of Truth, which sat encircled by the hollowed-out mountaintops of the Seven

Summits—the living quarters of the Truth Seekers—Daniel set a course for the southern continent and Camp Five. He placed the cargo pod on autopilot once he received his landing instructions, and sat back in the pilot's chair.

From the air, the refugee encampment was less than inviting. Rows of joyless shelters hugged the landscape. A light dusting of snow had settled on the frozen dirt roads running in between them. The few refugees who were brave enough to venture outside wore thick layers of ragged clothing, making their movements awkward as they hurried to get to where they were going.

The cargo pod circled around to find a landing spot, passing low over the temporary buildings and rattling the communications towers. Eventually, it set down on an empty patch of ground where a pair of greasy old anatoms were clearing up trash.

Daniel sat in the cockpit, staring out at the desolate shantyscape, and listened to the ice tinging on the glass.

It would be Luminara soon; that's what they kept telling him back at the Fortress of Truth, anyway. The galactic Festival of Light. He wasn't sure of the significance, but decorations had started going up everywhere and there was talk of some great feast to celebrate.

Feeble strings of lights stretched from tent to tent outside, bathing everything in a multicolored glow.

Daniel's stomach churned. He drummed his agitated fingers on the grimy controls. This was it? Dump and run?

Put a hundred kids into a tent no better than the wreck of that starship and wish them a nice life?

Daniel wanted to fire up the engines and get these kids out of here, but what was he going to do with them? Put them in the Seventh Summit where there was no one to take care of them?

Outside, a couple of Truth Seekers stepped out into the cold, pulling their bloodred cloaks tightly around their shoulders. One of them flicked through a holographic camp manifest as they trudged up to the pod.

Daniel didn't open the loading ramp until he heard them bang on the door. The servomotors whined as the metal slope lowered down onto the frozen-hard ground.

"You must be Daniel," one of the Truth Seekers announced, stepping into the pod.

He recognized her instantly. The long silver hair and inquisitive eyes of Juro the Doubting, one of the more formidable guardians serving on the Truth Seeker council. He hadn't expected someone so important to be here helping with refugees.

Regardless of her reputation, Daniel kept himself sandwiched between her and the huddled children behind him.

"Will they be safe here?" Daniel wanted to know.

"They will stay no longer than is necessary," Juro responded, not really answering the question. "At least fifteen will be gone by morning." She glanced over Daniel's shoulder and smiled at the children. "We've found some of their parents."

"Already?" Why did he have trouble accepting that?

Juro the Doubting squeezed the top of Daniel's arm. "You have done a great good today, Daniel. It's time for us to shoulder the burden now. If you'll let us."

Daniel swallowed hard. It didn't feel like he had done any good at all. It felt like he'd just given everyone a headache. He glanced back to see Tillowil and Kember and all the other children, shivering in the cold, uncertain of their future.

"I'm never going to see them again, am I?" he said.

"Who knows? One day perhaps, under happier circumstances," Juro replied warmly.

Daniel nodded and stepped aside, letting the two Truth Seekers shepherd the children down the ramp and onto ground that glistened with frost.

"Everyone stay together," Juro urged.

And they did.

9

SECRETS OF THE ORIGINARIUM

The hollowed-out mountain peak of the Seventh Summit appeared hunched against the starry night like a giant huddled around a campfire. Windows and construction lights twinkled at the ground levels—the sparks and embers at the giant's feet.

Once, this place had been left untouched, serving as a monument to the many Truth Seekers who had died in some terrible Sinja attack that had occurred years before Daniel's birth, when Tor Torin, the Keeper of Truth, had been a pupil here. Now life was returning. Anatoms and enginoids worked around the clock to restore the Seventh Summit to its former glory. And all because Daniel and a handful of other grubs had slipped the clutches of the Sinja and needed a home.

Six floors above the dormitory, inside an unfinished wing, Daniel followed the sound of bickering all the way to the doors of the room they called the Originarium, a place where the grubs gathered every clue to their origins and to the lives they must have known before the Sinja snatched them away and wiped their memories.

"I told you not to hook it up yet!"

That sounded like Henegan Rann.

Daniel stepped inside. Yes, it was Rann. Snatching one of the *Coldstar*'s data cores out of Fix Suncharge's hands before he could jam it into a receptacle, Rann snapped, "If we hook it up with power still running through it, we'll fry it."

Fix threw up his hands. "Sarree! Sarree!"

"It's 'sorry,'" Rann fumed, tinkering with the switches on a bunch of jury-rigged core readers he had looped together. "The word is 'sorry.' Saw-ree."

It was obvious Fix was really putting in an effort to speak Koin, the main language of the universe; he just couldn't get the hang of it. He'd mastered a few words but he couldn't string a sentence together. Koin was an odd language. It had evolved over thousands of years to serve as a common language between worlds, mostly for trade. It borrowed words and phrases from just about every language out there, but unless someone grew up with it, it was hard to make sense of the rules.

That was a clue in itself though, for Fix. How many

planets were there where Koin wasn't taught from birth? Not many.

Rann rubbed the back of his neck.

"Give him a break," Daniel said. "At least he's trying."

"Oh, look who showed up, the boy in the sparkles," said Rann.

The metal hexagons of Daniel's armored uniform definitely had a certain shine to them.

"Can you step away from the light, you're blinding me."

"You want a set of sleeks so bad? Join the Guild of Truth," Daniel retorted.

"And give up my freedom all over again? No thanks, pal," Rann scoffed.

Out of the four of them, Daniel was the only one who had become a Truth Seeker. Nails went back and forth on the idea. No one was sure what Fix thought. He knew he had the option, but he never talked about it.

All four of them had grown so much since their escape. Emotionally. Physically. Heck, Rann was now the tallest of the bunch; he'd sprouted almost overnight. Fix was at least two hands wider, and his legs were starting to look like they belonged on Alice. Even Daniel had changed. His skin had grown darker over time. He no longer had that unhealthy, pasty look of a life spent underground; his body had responded to even the merest hint of sunlight by turning a bronze color, somewhere between brown and olive.

But despite their emerging differences, they all shared

an experience that bound them to each other in ways that most people didn't understand. Taken as children, snatched from their families, their minds wiped clean.

Now they had the Originarium and its assorted collection of clues. A room where genetic data hung in the air like holographic decorations, where routes from planet to planet had been traced along the walls, revealing, for example, that only about five million people scattered throughout the galaxy had fingernails for hair. Each one of them could trace their ancestry back to a single family about two thousand years ago. They called themselves Yashkanars and didn't belong to one particular planet or star nation. They wandered endlessly. Most of them were geniuses with unparalleled technical skills in the sciences and mathematics, thanks to specially designed sections of DNA that the Yashkanars owned and would not sell to anyone outside of their clan. Their services were highly prized and they were paid handsomely for them. But they bored easily, and when they lost interest in their latest puzzle, they would move on.

"Where is Nails?" Daniel asked.

Bang!

"Ouch!" Nails cried, his voice muffled. "Jasper, watch where you put that flipper."

The penguin hummed a tune that sounded like an apology.

Rann nodded toward the computer array they had cobbled together at the other end of the room.

A gigantic hologram fizzed into existence; the wreck of the *Coldstar* nestled in the jungle on Oota Mheen. The three-dimensional image rotated slowly at the center of the room, right in front of them, the map Daniel had used to find it aligned perfectly.

"There!" Nails announced triumphantly. "I think we got it."

Daniel studied the projection of the ship as though seeing the *Coldstar* for the first time. "It's bigger than I realized," he said. It had broken in two when it crashed. The second piece sat a few miles away from the section Daniel had explored. "I wonder what I missed in that other half."

"Not much," said Rann, still tinkering with the data cores.

"I sure hope so," Nails remarked, climbing out from under the computer array. "Because he can't go back."

Rann fired up the first core. "There are star charts on here," he said. "And passenger logs." He eyed Daniel. "I wonder if you're listed."

It hadn't occurred to Daniel that he might have been a passenger aboard this ship. What an odd thought. And if he had been aboard, had his parents been there too? Were there security files tucked away somewhere with pictures of them?

A heavy weight pressed down on Daniel's shoulders, threatening to crush him. He shook his head, trying to clear it. "I wonder why it crashed?"

Fix held up a finger. "Pirates," he explained. It was only one word, but his pronunciation was pretty good. He brought up a holographic display of news reports that he had uncovered. The words floated in the air.

The *Coldstar*, owned and operated by the Neutron Star Line and flying the flag of Caresta, had been hosting a ten-day scientific symposium. Some of the brightest minds in the galaxy had gathered to share their latest discoveries when, about midway through its journey, it was attacked.

"It jumped to Inspinity," Daniel said, reading the reports aloud. "But its engines were badly damaged. It lost control and came down on Oota Mheen."

"About a thousand people died," Nails added.

"When did this happen?"

"About seven or eight years ago," Rann added.

Seven or eight years ago? Daniel would have been about five years old.

Fix nudged Nails. They chatted rapidly in Jarabic for a moment before Nails explained what was going on. Daniel really hated not knowing how to speak Jarabic.

"It gets weirder," Rann said. "The ship didn't even used to be called the *Coldstar*. It started out as the *Orion*—over fifty years ago. Fix says every time the ship was sold they changed its name."

"How long was it the *Coldstar*?"

"About a year."

Daniel shook his head. "I don't understand what any of

this has to do with me."

Rann rubbed his chin. "Whoever sent you that map seems to think it does. I wish someone would send me a map to *my* past."

"Ugh, the map," Daniel groaned. "That thing got me into a lot of trouble."

"Trouble?" Nails griped. "You could have been killed."

"Easier than trying to explain to everyone how I wound up out there."

"What?" Rann cut in. "You told them about the map?"

"Are you kidding me?" said Daniel. "Don't worry, nobody knows about the map."

From the doorway, Ionica's voice rang out. "We do *now*," she said. She sounded angry.

10

THE DEVIL IN THE DETAIL

Daniel gritted his teeth and kept his back to the door.

"What's wrong?" Ionica asked. "You assumed we were all too busy with the refugees to interrupt your little gathering?"

Ben and Astrid followed Ionica into the room. They didn't seem too happy either, though Astrid was eager to make sure everyone knew that her reasons were not the same as everyone else's. "I just came for Jasper," she said. "I can't believe I spent a year building that anatom and he likes Daniel more than he likes me."

Ben shrugged. "Everyone likes Daniel more than they like you."

Astrid held up a hand. "Yes. Thank you. Now if someone could just point me to my anatom. I don't really care about—*this* whole thing—"

"Shut up, Astrid," Ionica snapped.

"Now, wait a minute—"

Ben rested his hand on her shoulder.

Astrid huffed. "All right, all right."

Ionica marched over to Daniel, her force of personality so powerful that the other boys actually took a step back.

"We made a pact that we would help you find your families," she said simply. "We're not supposed to keep secrets from each other."

"It was necessary" was all Daniel said.

"Why?"

All of the former grubs refused to answer.

"Where did you get the map from?" Ben asked casually, coming over to check out the hologram.

"Someone sent it to Dan—" Rann explained before Daniel gave him a mean look to get him to quit yapping.

"*Who* sent it to you?" Ionica exploded.

"I don't know!" Daniel said defiantly. "I have no idea who sent me the map. It just showed up one day, right before we went to Oota Mheen."

Ionica's nostrils flared. *"How?"*

Nails stepped up, hands in his pockets. "It came in an anonymous comms message."

Ionica couldn't believe what she was hearing. "Did it ever occur to you that you were being led into a trap?"

"Of course," Daniel fired back.

"I would *never* have let you walk in there had I known."

64

"And that's why we didn't tell you!" Rann butted in. "Besides, you don't get to tell us what to do."

"It's not about telling you what to do. It's about saving your lives. It's about stopping you from getting yourselves killed."

"Well, guess what?" Rann snarled. "It wasn't a trap and we're not dead."

Ben scratched his head. "Can we please all just calm down? This is bonkers."

"Quite right," Astrid agreed. "Jasper? Come along, we're going!"

A sad-sounding cooing sound emerged from behind the computer array, followed by the waddling form of its owner, Jasper the anatomic penguin.

Astrid glanced down, inspecting the damage to her beloved creation on their way out. "What the Fuse happened to you?"

Jasper shrugged the question off with a quick flap of his flippers, as though he were embarrassed to be seen with his mother.

The remaining friends stood silently around the room, unable to look each other in the eye. Eventually Ben broke the ice. "Look," he said. "Obviously, someone went to a lot of trouble to make sure Dan knew there was a ship out there literally with his name on it. Whoever did it, and whatever their intentions were, we can't answer that right now."

"It's not about that," Ionica protested quietly. "It's about trust."

Rann threw up his hands and stomped straight through the hologram.

"Trust?" he said. "That's just it, none of you *Truth Seekers* trust us. Every time we get a hint of something that *might* help us figure out where we're from, you come up with excuses for why we can't go and see for ourselves."

"To keep you safe," Ionica argued.

"We can take care of ourselves," Rann shot back. "And I sure ain't sitting around here waiting for some family to magically show up. They probably think I'm dead already, if they're even out there at all."

Daniel wanted to make sure he understood what Rann was driving at. "Are you saying you want to leave?" he asked.

Rann straightened up. Shrugged. "Maybe."

"And go where?"

"You can't leave," Ionica insisted. "You'd never survive out there on your own."

Rann ignored her, turning to Nails and Fix.

"Why don't you come with me? We can't do any worse. We can head out with the refugees and start a new life."

Nails seemed genuinely torn. He discussed it briefly with a bewildered-looking Fix, but neither of them gave a definitive answer.

"What about you?" Rann asked, turning squarely on Daniel.

He could feel Ionica and Ben watching his every movement. For a fleeting moment it seemed so tempting, to strike out on his own again. Leave everything behind. But he'd made his choice, and besides, Ionica was right, the Sinja weren't finished with Daniel Coldstar. "I already pledged myself as a Truth Seeker," he said firmly.

Rann's face contorted as though some insect had just snuck up and stung him. "Well, I should have expected that, eh? Daniel Coldstar, Truth Seeker."

"Look," Daniel said. "Things are already better. We got out of the mines, didn't we?"

Henegan Rann thought it over. "Sure, we got out of the mines," he said. He tapped his head. "But we never got out of the mess."

Daniel couldn't argue with that.

He watched Rann walk away, knowing that whatever their differences, they both shared the same nightmares. He only hoped that Rann would realize that being with friends would make the memories easier to deal with than trying to cope alone.

11

HOW TO START A WAR

Over the next few days, classes resumed at the Fortress of Truth, and Daniel's life as a Beacon slowly approached normality, though he never felt truly at ease. Ionica, Ben, and Astrid seemed to have no such problem, but for Daniel, nothing felt right after everything he had seen on Oota Mheen. Maybe it got easier over time. He sure hoped so.

Zubenel Genubi was still as peculiar as ever, with his long mane of quills and his high-pitched helium-filled voice, which Daniel had learned sounded like that because there really was helium in Genubi's breathing mix. There were classes on advanced star lore, basic languages, and Igneous Schist's master class on planetary geology.

Then there were Captain Tinnell's lectures. Her classes had become so popular they were now virtually required. As an officer in the War Guild, she had insight into Sinja tactics and strategies that had become invaluable in trying to understand the chaos the galaxy was finding itself in. Daniel had finally started to understand that the guild's purpose was not to participate in war, but to understand, and to protect those not in a position to do so themselves.

Daniel watched Captain Tinnell stride confidently from one side of the floor to the other, cutting an imposing figure in her blue-and-white officer's uniform. He didn't know which planet she was originally from, but she was hairless. Not just bald, but devoid of any visible hair. No eyebrows. No eyelashes. Her forehead seemed forever furrowed and her steely gaze demanded that every Beacon pay attention.

Standing in the middle of the Forum, she began with a very simple question. "How do you start a war?"

Daniel shifted uneasily in his chair just as Tinnell turned around, looking straight at him. "You," she said. "What do you think?"

"Me?" Daniel said, startled. He'd assumed the question was rhetorical.

A room filled with a thousand Beacons and she picked him.

"Er, one side attacks the other," he said, groping for an answer. "The opponent retaliates. The situation escalates?"

Tinnell shrugged in agreement. "Simple, right?"

Daniel had the feeling he'd just walked into a trap.

"You were on Oota Mheen. Is that what happened there?" she asked.

How did she know that? What else did she know? Did

she know about the ship? Truth Seekers came and went as their missions dictated. She couldn't possibly have memorized everyone here.

Captain Tinnell watched him expectantly.

"No," Daniel replied. "The Sinja started the war on Oota Mheen."

"Are you sure about that?" she prodded. "The Sinja played no part in the battle."

"But they watched," Ben chipped in.

"If watching a war makes you a participant, then all of us here are guilty of the same. Correct?" she noted smoothly.

Ben threw himself back in his chair, defeated.

"How do you goad two sides into conflict? How do you get the people of both sides to actually *demand* a war?" Tinnell asked again, this time clearly not looking for the answers from her audience. "By gaining their trust. By pretending to be somebody you're not. Getting each side to believe that you are their ally. Whispering in their ears. Playing on their fear. And when the time is right—"

"Betray their trust," Daniel blurted out suddenly. He knew all about that. He had lived that.

"Exactly," Tinnell agreed. "We call them *agitators*. And it's a strategy the Sinja have used too many times before. That's what we're going to learn about today. Everyone, open your scrolls and turn to section one twenty-one."

Daniel reached into a pouch on the side of his kilt and joined the thousand other Beacons in rolling out his carbon polymer computing sheet with a familiar slap. The scroll, no thicker than a strand of hair, immediately projected a holographic view screen and created raised holocule controls around its edge.

"Sorry I'm late," Nails whispered, squeezing through and apologizing to every annoyed Beacon on his way to his seat in the row behind Daniel.

"You're very late," said Astrid.

"Yes, well, Fix and Rann had a lot to talk about this morning."

"But they didn't leave?" said Daniel.

"No, they're staying. For now." Nails unrolled his scroll. "What did I miss?"

"I'm trying to figure out how Captain Tinnell knew I was on Oota Mheen."

"I doubt there's a person in this room who doesn't know you were on Oota Mheen," Ionica scoffed. "Your reputation precedes you."

A small icon floated up into the air from one corner of Daniel's scroll. A message had arrived.

"Are you going to answer that?"

Reluctantly, Daniel let the single line of holographic text roll out in front of him. There was no sender's name attached.

How did you enjoy the ship?

Daniel shook his head. So now everyone knew about the *Coldstar*?

He composed a response. Great. Turns out I'm a prince and rich beyond my wildest dreams!

He glanced around the room, trying to spot whose scroll was about to light up with his reply. No one reacted. Their attention remained fixed on Captain Tinnell. Except for Astrid. Her eyes were bigger than moons.

"Really?" she said.

"Really what?"

"You're really a prince?"

Was that even an actual question? "No," he replied flatly, eager to turn his attention back to the lecture, only to find another message icon waiting for him.

He opened the next message. It read: Not true.

Not true? How would this joker know what was and wasn't true? Daniel studied the message ID. No name. There should be some kind of identifying information attached, but there wasn't. Where had this come from?

Who is this? Daniel demanded.

I'm the one who sent you the map, came the response. We should meet, don't you think?

Meet? A chill ran down Daniel's spine. He hadn't even considered that this person would want to meet.

Why would they want to meet? What did they want?

This was all spinning out of control.

12

BEING WATCHED

"This is a perfect example," Ionica said later, marching ahead and pushing through the crowd around the snow-covered Forum, "of why you should never have paid any attention to that map in the first place. This couldn't be a more obvious trap if they'd said *By the way, this is a trap.*"

Beacons everywhere were decorating for Luminara, pulling modified F-lights out of their cloak pockets and launching them into the air. The floating lights glowed yellow as they rose above everyone's heads, forming constellations of stars.

"Oh, give it a rest," Ben moaned, throwing a thick red cloak around his shoulders.

"I will not give it a rest," Ionica fired back.

Ben rolled his eyes. "Obviously."

Daniel walked six paces behind with Nails and Astrid,

keeping his head down and pulling his own cloak up around his neck.

"Oh, this is bad," Nails kept muttering. "This is really bad."

Astrid seemed oblivious. "Oh, I think they're rather pretty."

Nails shook his head. "What are you talking about?"

"The Luminara lights," she said with an uncertain smile. "What are *you* talking about?"

"You're unbelievable," Nails said, flabbergasted.

Astrid seemed to think that was the biggest compliment she'd ever heard. "Thank you, Matthew, that's so kind."

For a moment everyone wondered who she was talking about. So few people used Nails's real first name.

"The messages, Astrid. We're talking about the messages," he said.

"Oh, that," she said, brushing it aside. "Obviously someone's watching him. How else would they know he'd been to the ship? We'll just have to keep an eye out, that's all."

Everyone stopped in their tracks and turned on her.

"How do you know I'm being watched?" demanded Daniel.

"I don't," she said, so matter-of-factly that it was slightly unnerving. "It's implied. Someone asked how you liked the ship. Implying that they know you went to see it. Ergo, they know what you've been up to. So they are probably watching you. Why is this so difficult to understand?"

The implications racing through Daniel's brain were about to go supernova. "Astrid, that could mean a spy inside the Guild of Truth."

"Yes."

"But that's impossible."

"They're probably watching you right now," she added, glancing over her shoulder. "Or it could mean you're being tracked. You know?" She tapped a finger on the side of her head.

"My Identifier module . . . This is bad," Daniel sputtered. "This is really bad."

Ionica wanted to explode. "*Now* do you see what I was so worried about?"

A tornado of thoughts whirled around inside Daniel's brain so fast, his eyeballs started to hurt. For a moment he couldn't see, and he swayed on his feet. "I get it. I made a mistake, okay?" he said. "You'll never understand."

"Neither will you, apparently."

Ben eyed the faces in the crowd suspiciously, as though any one of them could be the spy. "What do we do?"

"Act normally," Astrid advised, her back stiffening. "Someone's coming over."

The overly excited Beacon rushing toward them had a shock of long black hair, gold-flecked skin, and a grin as wide as a nebula. "Only twelve more days to Luminara!" she said with gusto. "Happy Luminara! Did you bring your decorations?"

Daniel decided to get right to the point. "Who are you?" he asked flatly.

Her eyelids fluttered. "Kimato Daté,' she replied, perplexed by the reaction. When that didn't get a response, she added, "From Summit Six? FEE Club?"

Still nothing.

"Festivals and Events?"

Ben scratched his ear. "There's a club for that?"

"We don't have any decorations," Ionica explained coldly, clearly intending for that to be the end of the conversation and for Kimato to go away.

Kimato from FEE Club, on the other hand, seemed to think that was the saddest thing she'd ever heard. "I have a spare," she said, gently fishing out another light. "Would you like it?" The F-light glowed in her hand, a golden color that gently pulsated as though it were breathing.

Thankful for a way out of the awkward situation, Nails nodded frantically. "Yes, please!" he said. "Is there somewhere we need to be to launch it?"

"Well, right here is good—"

"No," Ionica responded coldly. "We're in the middle of something, and we need to discuss it—alone."

Kimato didn't quite know how to react. "I'm sorry," she muttered.

"I'm Nails," Nails cut in, shaking her hand vigorously. "Nice to meet you."

"Um, nice to meet you too?"

"Why don't we go over there and launch it," he suggested, guiding her away.

She flashed him a smile. "Okay," she said.

When they were sure she was out of earshot, Ben said, "What do we do now?"

Astrid made a pained expression as though she'd just eaten something that disagreed with her. "Perhaps," she said, "what if we can trace where these messages are coming from? That would give us an edge over this mysterious person."

"I don't see how," Daniel objected. "They're anonymous."

"Nothing's truly anonymous," Astrid explained. "Didn't you ever take Galactic Communications?"

"No."

"Node Coding? I must admit, Quotidian Borem isn't exactly the most exciting instructor this side of the galactic center, but he knows his stuff."

"Those are master-level classes," Daniel said. "How would we ever understand them?"

Astrid appeared taken aback. "I understood them."

"You took those classes?"

"Of course! They're really very simple."

"To *you*."

"You're wasting your time," Ionica said dismissively. "They're never going to get it, Astrid. What's your plan?"

"Now wait a minute," Ben objected.

"Be quiet and listen," Ionica shot back.

"Right. Daniel," Astrid said, "display the messages."

Reluctantly, Daniel slid his hand in an arc in front of his chest. His holographic control panel fizzed into the air, each message represented by a separate icon.

In all cases the icons read: S E N D E R   U N K N O W N.

"See?" Ben said.

Astrid dismissed him. "No, look here," she explained, pointing out the routing information being displayed as text in one corner of the scroll. "This tells you which node each message came from."

"What's a node?" asked Daniel.

Astrid looked as though she wanted to scream. "Does anyone here know how interstellar communications work?"

"No!" everyone cried in unison.

Astrid took a deep breath. "Okay, look," she said. "When somebody sends a message, they are at Point A. And when someone receives a message, they're at—"

"Point B," Ben replied, irritated.

"No! They're not at Point B at all! They're at Point Z," Astrid explained, trying her best to remain calm. "Tiny brains," she muttered to herself. "Tiny brains. How do I explain this?" She took another moment, then said, "Galactic communications travel through all these little points called nodes. The first node is Point A, then it goes to Point B, then C, then D, and so on until it reaches you."

"How many nodes are there?"

"Millions."

Daniel shrugged. "Why?"

"What do you mean *why*? What a ridiculous question."

Ben scratched his head. "He's got a point."

Exasperated, Astrid tried to explain. "If you just had two nodes, one at Point A and one at Point B, how would you talk to other places? You need a network. And if one part of the network gets damaged, you need a way to reroute the communication, so you need what's called *redundancy*!"

"But how does that help us?" Daniel wondered.

Astrid called up a holographic map of the galaxy from her scroll and had it float in the air between them. "Each node adds a code to the message, letting the next node in the chain know where it came from. These codes tell you which star the node is orbiting for a whole slew of reasons that involve quantum entanglement, which I already regret saying out loud." She waved a hand as though clearing the thought away. "Forget I said anything, just activate the code on the scroll."

Daniel did as instructed. Immediately, each star in the galactic hologram pulsed individually, one at a time.

"What's it doing?"

"It's comparing the code to each known star code registered throughout the galaxy. There are trillions for each star. Every time the star has a hiccup or burps out solar radiation, the code changes to let other nodes know what to do if the message gets scrambled in transmission."

"This is making my head hurt," Daniel said.

"Just imagine what it felt like to the woman who invented all of this," Astrid said. "All you need to know is that these codes are like breadcrumbs. And if we follow these breadcrumbs, eventually they will lead us all the way back to the planet of origin."

After a moment the scroll found a match. The star associated with the node code changed color.

"There," she said. "Periss."

"That's where the message comes from?" Ben asked.

Astrid clamped her eyes shut. "Have you been listening to a word I've been saying?"

"Yes."

"Well, obviously not!" She took a breath. "Periss is the last node it passed through. Now we look for the node before that, and the node before that. And we do that for each message until, theoretically, we work our way back to the first one—its point of origin."

Daniel laughed. "How many are there?"

"Thousands," Ionica commented. "At least. This could take days."

"Probably weeks," Astrid explained.

"And what if the point of origin is different for each message?" Ionica asked.

"Then our sender is moving throughout the galaxy, and I have no idea how to track them."

Daniel chewed on everything he had just learned. This

was all so complicated. "What does it matter where the messages came from?"

Astrid blinked. "What are you talking about?"

"We're overthinking it," he said. "What matters is where this person wants to meet."

Ionica couldn't believe it. "You're not actually thinking about doing this?"

Daniel brought the sender's last message back up—We should meet, don't you think?—and sent a reply before anyone could stop him; one simple word: Where?

The four friends waited impatiently, while the snowflakes grew thick and heavy.

Eventually, the response came.

Juba, it said.

Ionica looked as though she'd been kicked in the gut.

"What is it? What's so bad about Juba?" said Daniel. When she wouldn't answer, he looked to Ben and to Astrid, but they were silent, waiting for Ionica to explain.

"Tell me," Daniel urged.

"Juba's my home," she said.

13

TORIN'S PLAN

Beneath the feet of where the Seven Summits met, locked within a subterranean honeycomb of burnished tritanium beams, sat the grand repository of all Truth Seeker knowledge—the Vault of Truth.

The Vault bustled with students poring through holocule textbooks hanging like leaves from the data trees, some obviously only doing so to stay out of the cold. Orpheus Core's winters were notoriously long and brutal.

Daniel, Ionica, Astrid, and Ben sullenly weaved their way through, past the great glass chamber where the Book of Planets used to sit. Its infomatic still displayed a picture of its discoverer—the famed explorer Vilé Sa—and an explanation on the value of the book, as though Keeper Torin fully expected the ancient tome to be returned to its rightful place someday.

They climbed the steps to the workshops and Tor Torin's chambers.

Daniel's heart hammered in his chest. He took a deep breath when he reached the Keeper's door, preparing himself to see the disappointment in Torin's eyes when he learned the truth.

He knocked loudly.

"Come in!" Tor Torin replied.

The heavy door slid open.

"Have you ever noticed," Tor Torin said, "that in order to dislodge something from between your teeth, you have to insert something else between your teeth?"

Keeper Tor Torin seemed positively awestruck by this revelation. He stood behind his artifact-laden desk, only his pewter hair visible, which bobbed about whenever he moved.

"Hello," Daniel replied, ignoring the question entirely. The others followed him into the room and stood quietly beside him.

Torin poked his head out from behind one of his many towers of stuff. "Ah, there you are, at last."

"You weren't looking for me," Daniel reminded him. "I was looking for *you*."

"And yet *I* found *you*!" Torin insisted, rounding his desk to reveal that besides his Truth Guardian robes, he wore a pair of pink fluffy slippers. "On the other side of *my* desk, no less! Even though I wasn't even looking for you. That's the beauty of relativity! Ten thousand years later and it's as true as ever. Two different perspectives, two equally valid descriptions of one event!"

Ionica coughed politely. "Keeper Torin," she cut in. "We have something to tell you."

"I certainly hope so," Torin replied with a mischievous twinkle in his eye. "I can't imagine you came here just to stand about." He turned back to Daniel, looking up at him expectantly. "Did you? Did you come here just to stand about?"

There was a time when Daniel and Tor Torin could look each other right in the eye, but that time had passed. Daniel had grown several inches since they first met, while Torin, who had once been Daniel's age, well over a hundred years ago now, would never achieve such giddy heights.

Daniel looked down on him.

"You've grown," said Torin. "That's quite annoying." Easing up into a large wingback chair that looked like it had been covered in the spiky green skin of a durian fruit, he said, "I suppose you'd better tell me all about this ship." His feet dangled back and forth.

Ben groaned. "You know about the ship?"

"Of course. What an odd question," Torin mused. "Very little happens around here without my knowing about it."

Daniel considered that statement. "So you know about the map."

Torin looked uncomfortable. Maybe even embarrassed. "What map?" Intrigue and concern played across his face.

In a calm, measured voice, he said, "Daniel. What's going on?"

Daniel's heart sank. He closed his eyes. How in the world was he going to explain this one to Tor Torin of all people? His mentor. The closest thing to a father that he had any memory of.

"It's really quite simple," Astrid explained, bubbling with excitement and speaking twice as fast as she needed to. "You see, Daniel got sent this map, *completely* anonymously, that told him where to find a ship in the jungles of Oota Mheen called the *Coldstar*. *Obviously* not a coincidence. So he goes there and winds up finding a group of children about to be enslaved by the Sinja! And Daniel thinks, that's odd, something like that happened *to me*. So later he gets another anonymous message asking him how he liked the ship, because apparently this is the same person who sent the map, and Daniel says something like *How did you know I was on the ship?* And they go back and forth, and eventually the person on the other end says, *Well, don't you think we ought to meet?* And Daniel says, *Sure, where?* And they say—*Juba.* . . ."

An uncomfortable silence fell over the room while Torin tried to digest what he had just heard.

Awkwardly, Astrid attempted to ease the tension. "It's all very exciting."

Torin held up a hand. "Yes. Yes, I get it."

Ionica took a deep breath. "Keeper Torin," she said. "Juba is my home. I was also there at the ship with Daniel.

I think I'm connected to this in some way."

"Could just be a coincidence," Torin pondered, settling back into his chair.

"Guardian Alioth says there's no such thing as coincidence," Daniel said.

"Spoken like someone who has obviously never experienced one," said Torin, before pretending to catch himself. "Oh, I'm sorry, was that out loud?"

Like an insatiable engine of curiosity, Torin sprang out of his chair. "Tell me, what have you found out about who has been sending you these messages?"

Ben shrugged. "Not much."

"I think it's all a trap," Ionica explained.

"Possibly," Torin mused. "But to what end? If it's a trap, why didn't they spring it on Oota Mheen?"

"They tried. The Tarafand forces nearly wiped us out."

"That's rather elaborate, don't you think? For someone who poses little threat to the Sinja now that they have the Book of Planets and have fled Musa Degh, to divert an entire squad of Thunderheads to kill Daniel in the middle of their very important war?"

"The Thunderheads are working with Vega Virrus," Daniel pointed out. "They said so."

Torin agreed. "I'm sure they are. They were there for the children who you rescued. By the sound of things, you were an unexpected inconvenience."

"Keeper Torin," Ben countered thoughtfully, "if they

didn't tell the Sinja that Daniel visited that ship, then it has to be a spy, or he's being tracked. Otherwise how would this—whoever it is—know that he had been there?"

"A fine question, Mr. Quick." Torin held out his hand to Daniel. "May I read these messages?"

Daniel pulled up his holographic display and flicked the icons across the room to his mentor.

The holograms unfurled before his eyes and Torin read them with interest. "These are vague enough that they could be a complete guess," Torin noted. "A shot in the dark just in case you really had gone to see it. I doubt very much that there is a spy following your every move." He wiped the messages away. "As for your being tracked, I doubt it, but it's possible, what with your Identifier and all."

Ionica looked uncomfortable. "Actually, I track him all the time. He tends to get into all sorts of trouble, you know," she said.

Daniel gestured to Torin. "See? It's like living under a microscope. I need this thing out of my head. Especially with everything going on." He rounded on Astrid. "What about that device you were working on? The trans—transparent scintillator—"

"Transductive Oscillator," Astrid corrected.

"Will that work?"

"I have no idea. It might. Or it might do nothing at all. Or it might work but there are terrible side effects. I haven't even begun to test it yet."

"You said you'd used something like it before."

"Yes," she replied. "But not on a person!"

Torin beamed with excitement. "You've been working on using a Transductive Oscillator *on a person*?"

"Yes," Astrid admitted.

"That's really quite brilliant!"

"I know," Astrid agreed immodestly.

"I've been waiting for the day I might meet a Beacon half as smart as me, and you may well be *half* as smart as me!"

Astrid narrowed her eyes. "Thank you?" she said.

"Let's work on this together and see if we can't get it to work," Torin added, pacing back and forth. "Tell me about Juba," he asked Ionica. "What do we know about it? What's so special about your home?"

"I'm from the city of Vespertine," she said. "We have Traders Wharf—it's a trading post. But not even the biggest one in that arm of the galaxy. We're more of a stopping-off point on the way to somewhere else rather than a destination."

"Then why do people go to Juba at all?"

"They don't," Ionica replied. "Not usually. Except for the next couple of weeks."

Torin shot her a look. "What's so special about the next couple of weeks?"

A light flickered in Ionica's eyes. "Luminara," she said.

Torin spun on his heel. "Luminara!" he cried.

Daniel held up his hand. None of this was making any

sense to him. "I thought Luminara was celebrated by the whole galaxy?"

"Not the *whole* galaxy," Torin explained. "But a lot of it."

"So why does it make any difference if it's Luminara on Juba too?"

"Because this year it's Juba's turn to bear witness."

"Bear witness? To what?"

"Daniel," Torin asked thoughtfully, "do you even know what Luminara is? It's a symbol of peace. We celebrate it to remind ourselves of the havoc that war can wreak. Ironic, considering the state of our galaxy today. Many thousands of years ago, humans fought each other in a savage war, in a distant star system. A war so brutal, and so without mercy, that the host star and all of its planets were destroyed in a wave of destruction rivaling a supernova," Torin lamented. "The light from that blast was so intense that just like the light of the stars, it has been traveling throughout the galaxy ever since."

"This year," Ionica added, "the light will reach Juba, and we will witness that past destruction for ourselves."

Torin quickly disappeared behind his desk and started fiddling with his projects. "But the meaning is almost completely lost now. There are Beacons in this very fortress who arrive not even knowing the name of the planet that perished or its significance. Last year, I swear I heard someone call it Dirt."

"What *is* the name of the planet?"

"It's Earth, Daniel," Torin explained, emerging from the other side of his desk. "It's the birthplace of mankind. It's where we took our first steps. Where civilizations were first built. Where pyramids soared and our ancestors were buried. And all of that is gone. All we are left with is the light, and even that is starting to fade."

"I don't understand what any of this has to do with us," Daniel remarked.

"Catch," Torin said, producing a small object from behind his back and tossing it to Astrid. "A delineator. It'll help with the oscillator."

Astrid reacted like she'd just been handed a birthday present. "Thank you!" she said.

"All right. Where was I?"

"Luminara," Ionica reminded him.

"Right!" Torin said. He steepled his fingers in front of his lips. "Luminara attracts pilgrims. Hundreds of thousands of them. From all over the galaxy. People from all walks of life. Strange faces in the crowd will not draw attention. Getting lost in the crowd would certainly provide cover for a meeting. A very smart use of Luminara, to ask you to meet on Juba. That tells me they are serious about this meeting."

"You want us to go there?" said Daniel, astonished.

"Isn't that a little dangerous?" Ionica protested.

"Very."

"How would I even know where to look?" Daniel argued.

"You don't look," Torin explained. "I suspect they will

come to you. All you will have to do is hide in all the right places and wait. I suggest we grant Ionica official leave to go home for the holidays, and that it just so happens she takes you with her."

"What about my Identifier?" Daniel protested. "If they're tracking me, no crowd is going to give *me* any cover."

"We will work that out," Torin assured him. "Astrid and I will come up with a solution."

Astrid seemed perplexed. "Why? I've already got most of it figured out."

Torin seemed taken aback. "All right. Then I will assist you."

Astrid shrugged. "If it'll make you feel better."

Torin took a deep breath. "Touché."

Ben rolled his eyes.

"Wait a minute," Ionica said. "I'm not doing this if it will endanger my family."

"Well, of course not," Torin replied confidently. "We have Seekers everywhere. You will not be alone on Juba. We *will* be watching over you, but from the shadows. We don't want to scare this mysterious person off."

"Scaring them off isn't what I'm afraid of," said Daniel. "Making them angry is. What then?"

If Tor Torin had an answer to calm Daniel's very real fear, he wasn't sharing it.

14

TWILIGHT ON JUBA

Juba was a peculiar-looking planet.

One side faced the sun continuously, so it never had a chance to cool down. Its scorching temperatures were over a thousand degrees higher than the frigid temperatures at its other side, which never saw daylight and sat in permanent subzero darkness. This left just a narrow band of twilight stretching vertically from north to south that remained habitable.

"What's that?" Daniel asked, mesmerized by the clusters of lights dotting the narrow strip.

"Our equator," Ionica explained. "It's the only place where anyone can live. The cities all blur into one."

"It's beautiful."

"It is now," she said. "Just wait until stormy season."

Whenever the hot air and cold air of the two hemispheres met, incredible storms rolled around the equator, forcing everyone to shelter in place.

Stormy season. Daniel's mood darkened. What were they about to walk into down there? "It'll be fine," he kept saying, trying to reassure himself. "It'll be fine."

"If Keeper Torin thinks this will work, who am I to argue?" Ionica commented.

"If you're that worried about it," Daniel said, "you should have told him."

"I *did* tell him." A light flashed on the controls. "Okay," she said. "Plug in, this could get bumpy."

She wasn't kidding. When Ionica punched the controls allowing the Air-Drive to detach from the caravan hauler and join the preprogrammed convoy down to the equator's surface, the vehicle shook violently.

From one of the rear compartments, the sound of something smashing against the pressure door grabbed their attention. Daniel craned his neck to see Jasper rolling out into the passageway behind them, squealing. The mechanical penguin staggered to his webbed feet and shook his head.

Daniel couldn't believe it. "Jasper!" he barked angrily. "What are you doing here?"

The anatom made some kind of tuneless noise that didn't explain anything.

Daniel threw himself back in his chair, watching the

Air-Drives in front of them in the convoy peel off in different directions. "We really have to give him a proper voice
box or we're never going to know what he's saying."

"You're sure you want to mess with Astrid's pride and
joy?" Ionica asked. "Good luck with that."

"Oh no," he said. "She's going to be so mad when she
realizes he wandered off again."

Before long, it was their turn to peel off and follow a trail
of Air-Drives along the route to Vespertine, Ionica's home
city. Air-Drives were only equipped with sub-light engines.
They could reach orbit but they were too small to house
faster-than-light engines, so most people got around the
galaxy this way, by renting space on caravan haulers that
transported them to their destination. The Air-Drives came
in all sorts of shapes and sizes. The one Torin had arranged
for them had a couple of beds and a bathroom in case they
needed to live out of it for any length of time.

Daniel *really* hoped it wouldn't come to that.

As the Air-Drive dove down over the equator, the skies
dimmed to a purple twilight; bright yellows and orange
streaked the sky on one horizon, blackest night twinkled
with stars on the other, while the clouds were filled with
sky trawlers, floating fishing boats with solar sails that
dredged for balloon-like animals called shamashi that lived
in Juba's atmosphere.

Daniel could have heard Ionica's stomach growling from
the other side of the planet. "You eat those things?"

"They're a delicacy!" she said, watching the hydrogen-filled creatures shoot flames between their fronds. She explained that they did this to both move about and attract birds and insects into their clutches. "Oh, I hope my family has some at home."

"How long has it been since you were home?" Daniel asked delicately. In all the time he had known Ionica, she had either been taking classes at Orpheus Core or out on missions. He couldn't remember her ever going home.

She glanced down wistfully. "Too long," she said. "It's been too long." And left it at that.

They landed at a parking structure in the middle of one of Vespertine's many sprawling bazaars. Its mazelike streets and alleys were jam-packed with people from all over the galaxy. It was only on the ground that Daniel realized that the markets didn't just sprawl out around him, but were stacked, nestled into narrow canyons and connected by flimsy bridges.

They both wore civilian clothes to blend in, though they had packed their uniforms just in case. Daniel wore a jacket and a black pair of pants, with a shirt that didn't seem to fit correctly because he still had his Aegis pinned to his chest underneath it. A year later and he still couldn't take the relic off.

Ionica wore a bold tangerine dress and knee-high boots. Daniel had never seen her out of Truth Seeker sleeks before. She looked . . . different.

"I hope Keeper Torin has us under observation, or we're not even going to make it home," she said.

Daniel scanned the crowd. Any strange face could be a threat here. "I'm not sure they'd make their move now," he said. "Not when we just got here."

"And you're suddenly an expert?"

"It's just a feeling," he said, scratching his chest.

"Well," Ionica replied. "I don't trust your feelings."

He scratched again. The angular parts of his Aegis, hidden beneath his shirt, poked at the fabric.

"Why don't you just take it off like everyone else?" she said, exasperated.

"I *can't* take it off," Daniel said.

"You've been wearing it for a year. It's like a comfort blanket. I don't even know how you get dressed."

"With difficulty," he replied.

A dozen paces behind them, Jasper did his best to keep up. Constantly distracted by the spices, perfumes, fabrics, and roasted drotes on sticks, the anatom trembled when he ran straight into the legs of a gigantic dark figure wrapped in a ragged cloak.

The anatom let out a low rumble that immediately alerted the two Beacons.

Daniel turned back to find the figure peering down at the quaking penguin through a mouthless mask, with deep-set eyes that were nothing more than unblinking holes.

"Jasper," Ionica beckoned, trying to remain calm. "Come

on, just get out of its way."

The anatom followed the instructions as best he could, shakily stepping aside to let the ghastly figure pass.

"When did they start letting Purgents come to Juba?" Ionica wondered, watching the mute figure disappear into the crowd.

"*That's* a Purgent?" Daniel muttered.

He'd heard about them, but he'd never seen one before. Instead of being exiled on Felonis, or some other prison planet, these prisoners, thieves for the most part, elected to work off their crimes by promising to purge themselves of their misdeeds. Their minds were transferred to robotic bodies while their actual bodies were kept in stasis pods at a secure facility. One wrong action and a Purgent's robotic body would shut down permanently and they would die.

"I'd rather go to Felonis than become that," said Daniel.

For once, Ionica refrained from some witty comeback. "It's not the Purgent that bothers me," she said. "It's its master. Sometimes their idea of doing good is not the same as yours or mine, and the imprisoned soul has to follow those orders regardless."

"Doesn't somebody check to make sure masters are good people before letting them take charge?"

"No. Anyone can be a master," she explained. "All they have to do is pay off the Purgent's debts and sign a contract."

"That's it?"

"That's it." She glanced around, checking to make sure there weren't any other surprises waiting for them. "Come on," she said.

They took a public shuttle across town and arrived at a residential district about an hour later.

The Lux family house sat at the end of a cul-de-sac, surrounded by tall, purple-leafed Rurbidon trees. A beat-up old Clodhopper sat out front, looking like a headless bird standing on its two rear landing legs. With peeling red paint and a dinged-up body and folded stabilizer wings, it wasn't fancy like the Air-Drive sitting in the garage, but it looked in good enough shape to fly the Lux family around Juba when they needed to travel.

"What's your dad's name again?" Daniel asked nervously.

"Mimias."

"I think I'll just stick to Mr. Lux," he said. "And who's Dimas?"

"Dimas is my youngest brother. Joules is my other brother."

They were almost at the house now, walking up a stony embankment dotted with thorny desert scrub.

"Anyone else I should know about?"

"Mom, of course. And my sister," Ionica said, tensing up. "But we don't talk about her, okay?"

"Okay."

"You promise?"

This was the first he'd even heard of her. Why would he want to upset Ionica? "I promise," he said.

They followed the path all the way to the entrance. Why did he feel so nervous? Why did he hope they liked him? A whirl of strange thoughts he had never even considered before today bounced around inside his head like colliding asteroids.

"Families are complicated," he said.

"You have no idea," Ionica replied, opening the front door.

15

NOBODY EXPECTS
THE LUX INQUISITION

"Hello?" said Daniel, poking his head around the door.

Ionica had just hurried into the house. Was she ever coming back? What was he supposed to do now?

It occurred to him that he had never been inside somebody's home before now. Living quarters at Truth Seeker complexes, sure; government buildings, judicial centers, starships. But not a home.

Should he go inside?

Awkwardly, he stepped over the threshold and stood on the rug by the potted plants in the entranceway. The house had a completely different feel than anywhere he'd ever been before. It was inviting. He could smell food cooking.

What was he supposed to do in somebody's home? Sit

down? There was a chair in the corner. Wander off on his own? Wait for somebody to notice him? Why was this so difficult?

"This is weird," a boy said, walking around Daniel and looking at him like he was on display in a museum.

Where had he come from?

"What's weird?" Daniel asked uneasily.

"I don't think my sister ever brought a *boy* home before," he said.

"She must have," Daniel countered. "She has friends."

"Not those kinds of friends," the boy said, wandering off.

"What's that supposed to mean?" Daniel called after him, but he was long gone. Which one was he? The younger brother, or the younger younger brother?

"Hey, what's this?" a small voice asked off to the side. He was a smaller boy. *This* had to be the younger younger brother. The kid couldn't be any older than five. He held Jasper by the beak and kept lifting one of his flippers up and down.

"It's an anatom," Daniel explained.

"Yeah, but what is it?"

"A penguin."

"What's a penguin?"

Good question. "I don't know," Daniel admitted. "They just told me it's a penguin."

"You're weird."

The little boy wandered off to a new distraction. Jasper

made a move like he was going to snap at the kid, but Daniel wagged a finger.

"Don't you even think about it," he warned.

"Who might you be?" a tall pale man with a deep voice asked. He had gray-and-black hair and stepped through from the garage, cleaning gunk off his hands with a rag.

"Uh, Daniel Coldstar, sir," Daniel replied uncertainly.

This *had* to be Ionica's father, Mimias Lux.

"Huh," the man said. It was difficult for Daniel to tell what that reaction meant. Mimias turned to head deeper into the house and called over his shoulder, "Well, don't just stand there, come on in, young man." He gave a quick twitch of his head for Daniel to follow. "You can leave your bag by the stairs."

Daniel did as he was told, dutifully following along behind. Was he supposed to say something? What was he supposed to do?

"Kyra!" Mimias called out as they neared the kitchen. "I found *this* by the door. I don't think it's one of ours."

It took a moment for Daniel to realize that he was talking about *him*.

"We'll be right there," Ionica's mother replied, her voice unsteady.

"Well, grab a seat," Mimias said, jabbing a finger at the dining table. "You're just in time for dinner."

Daniel did as he was told, and Ionica's father wandered off, leaving him all alone again. What the heck was he supposed to do now? Just sit here?

This was all so strange.

Before long an anatom came in and started setting the table and laying out the food, while Mimias called upstairs for Dimas and Joules to get their butts in their chairs before they made him come up there. Whatever that meant.

The boys ran downstairs before it could be explored further.

When Ionica took her seat at the table opposite Daniel, she gave him a disapproving look.

"We don't let anyone sit in that chair," she whispered.

"I'm sorry, I didn't know," Daniel spluttered, abruptly getting up and scooting onto the next chair over.

When Ionica's mother sat down at the other end of the table, looking flustered, she jumped when she noticed Daniel.

"Oh, good grief," she said. "I'd forgotten we had a visitor."

Mr. Lux looked at his wife like that was the craziest thing he'd heard all day. "I *just* told you."

She turned to Daniel. "Ionica tells me you're David?" she asked, trying to sound polite.

"Mom . . ."

"Daniel. Daniel Coldstar, ma'am," he said.

"Huh," she said. And then, after a long while, said, "Can someone pass me the pottereens?"

Daniel glanced over at Ionica, hoping for some reassurance that everything was all right, but it never came. She looked different somehow. Was it because her hair was down, which it rarely ever was? Or was it because he'd never seen her around her parents—

She glared at him, probably wanting him to stop staring.

Dimas Lux, who had been watching the whole thing, gave a sly grin. "Daniel is Ionica's boyfriend."

"I knew it!" Joules cried.

Daniel looked down at his food, embarrassed.

Ionica slapped her little brother on the wrist. "He is not my boyfriend!"

"Then why is he here?" Joules asked.

"Because he has no one to spend Luminara with and I thought it might be a nice thing to do," Ionica snapped. "Don't be so rude."

"He's a bit weird," Dimas added.

Ionica raised her hand again. Her father didn't even look up from his plate. "Stop hitting your brother."

Ionica pulled her hand away, but she did not look happy about it. "Then tell him to stop it."

"Dimas, stop it," Mimias said in between chews.

"No," Dimas protested.

"He says no," Mimias announced, breaking off a piece of litlik bread.

Ionica folded her arms and sat back in her chair.

Daniel had never seen anything like it. What in the world was going on? Was this how families really acted? And Ionica, someone he had always seen as fierce and independent—she was totally different here.

"So where are you from, Daniel?" Ionica's mother asked.

"I don't know," Daniel replied. "Not originally, anyway."

"He was a slave of the Sinja," Ionica hurriedly explained. "We're trying to find his parents."

"Oh, how horrible," her mother said.

Mimias Lux grunted by way of a response. And then, after a couple of thoughtful chews, added, "So you're the reason we have Truth Seekers stationed outside my house?"

Daniel didn't know how to react.

"Father, how do you know about that?" Ionica said, stunned.

"I work for the Defense Directorate, young lady. I wouldn't be very good at my job if I didn't know that much." He winked. "Also, they told me."

Was this why Torin was so confident of their safety? "So you're a Truth Seeker too, sir?" Daniel asked.

Mimias dismissed him with a snort. "I'm an engineer."

"We both are," Kyra Lux added.

"The only Truth Seeker ever to come out of this family is that one," he said, jerking a thumb at his daughter.

"I see," Daniel said, downcast. "I just assumed . . ." His voice trailed off.

"Assumed what? That it's a family business? A kind of destiny? No. We all make our own choices and our own mistakes in this family."

Daniel shot Ionica a quizzical look. "Then why did *you* become a Truth Seeker?"

Ionica coughed. "It doesn't matter," she said.

"We lost her big sister some time ago," her mother explained. "It changed all of us. The boys were too young to understand, but Ionica . . ." Now her voice trailed off.

Ionica had specifically asked Daniel not to talk about her sister and now it was happening anyway, and it was sort of his fault.

An Aegis would have a hard time cutting the tension in this room.

Joules pushed his food around his plate. "I don't like this," he said. "Can I have dessert?"

"Just eat your dinner!" both parents snapped at roughly the same time.

The two Lux parents eyed each other across the table, having what seemed like a telepathic conversation, because although they didn't say a word, they seemed to understand each other.

After dinner, they showed Daniel to his room in a wing as far away from the family bedrooms as possible. Jasper hefted Daniel's bag inside and stuffed it into a closet, and after that, he and the anatom were left alone.

The immense room had a portrait of an older lady hanging on one wall; her stern face gazed down at him disapprovingly. There were trinkets hanging on another wall—a ceremonial horn and a headscarf. Pipes that could have been a musical instrument or part of an engine; Daniel wasn't sure.

Left to his own devices, Daniel also wasn't quite sure what to do with himself. He sat on the edge of the lumpy bed.

"So this is what it's like to have a family, huh?" he said.

Jasper shrugged, as if to say, *How the heck should I know?* Then proceeded to open any drawer he could find and inspect its contents.

"Jasper, I don't think you should be doing that."

The anatom dragged out a dusty old trophy dedicated to Ionica Lux, first place, long jump. He tossed it away and resumed rummaging around some more, humming away to himself.

"Jasper, stop!" Daniel ordered.

The anatom reluctantly did as he was told, shaking his head and extending his neck with disapproval.

The icy stare of the lady in the painting bored down on them both.

Restless, Daniel fished his scroll out of his bag and made himself comfortable on the bed. He opened it up, composed a message to Ionica, and sent it.

All it said was: I'm sorry.

Daniel would have left it at that. He hadn't expected Ionica to reply.

It's okay, she messaged back.

After a while, she wrote again.

Are you ready for tomorrow? It's going to be really dangerous.

I'm nervous, Daniel admitted.

Nervous? I'm scared out of my mind, Ionica replied.

Well, I have other issues to deal with.

Like what?!

I don't think the lady in this picture likes me very much, Daniel replied.

Oh, that's my grandmother, Ionica said. She didn't like anybody. My sister used to call her the Star-Witch.

Haha.

Daniel held on to his smile as long as he could, but his curiosity kept bubbling to the surface. Eventually, he said, What happened to her?

My grandmother?

Your sister.

What part of "I don't want to talk about it" don't you understand?

The "don't" part. Daniel could just hear her rolling her eyes. I'm hungry, he said.

We just had dinner.

Yeah, hours ago.

Unreal.

Daniel waited for her to say something else, but nothing came for a few minutes.

So do you have any snacks? he said.

I'm getting them!

Oh.

Meet me up on the deck.

16

UNDER THE STARS

"I'm not sure we should be out here," Daniel said, feeling uncomfortable.

Like much of the architecture on Juba, the Lux household's deck was disk-shaped, extending out from the roof at the back of the house. It offered a great view of the city, but it was so exposed it wouldn't take long for somebody to notice, say, a human target, sitting around like he was just waiting to be snatched.

"It's okay," Ionica assured him. "We have a Prism. No one can see us up here. Just keep your voice down before you wake the whole house." She smoothed the wrinkles out of her blanket and dumped the snacks she'd taken from the kitchen on it.

Daniel had seen Prisms in action before: security grids

that scattered the light so that it appeared as though structures were empty when in fact they were teeming with people—usually soldiers. Prisms were military-grade technology.

"You know there's a table and chairs right over there," Daniel said, plopping himself down.

"I can't lie down and look at the stars in a chair," Ionica scoffed. She pulled open a bag of puffy-looking balls of something. They had a crispy golden shell but looked soft in the center as she ate them.

"What are those?"

"Loukoumades."

Daniel remained suspicious. "Are they any good?"

"Awful," she said, popping another one in her mouth. She grinned.

Daniel reached over and grabbed one from the foil bag. He examined it. Sniffed it.

"You don't have to eat it. No one's got a blaser to your head."

"Today," said Daniel.

He took a small bite. "Nasty," he said, savoring the sweet flavor. "I'd better make sure I really don't like them." He grabbed a handful.

They sat with their backs against a huge rectangular planter watching the ships flit against the twilight sky. A warm breeze carried the sweet scent of ripe mothbean.

"I wonder who it is," Daniel mused.

"You mean who you're supposed to meet?"

"Yeah."

"I don't think it matters who," said Ionica. "I think it matters *why*."

"Sometimes there is no why," he said, scratching around the snacks, looking for anything else that looked interesting. "I don't know why the Sinja took me, and I don't think I'll ever find out."

"Then why are you meeting this—whoever they are—if you don't think it's going to help?"

"Because the map led me to something real. For the first time, something I might have a connection to," Daniel explained. "I'll listen to whoever this is. It doesn't mean what they have to say will be true. I've learned that much as a Seeker. But I'll listen. Then maybe I'll get to ask why."

"Why what?"

"Why any of this happened. Why I was taken in the first place."

Ionica suppressed a smile, but even that small tug on her lips soon faded. "I wish I had someone to ask why. Why did my sister have to die," she said.

Daniel's ears pricked up. He had questions, so many questions, but he wasn't about to start pushing. He kept his mouth shut. If she wanted to talk, she'd talk.

They ate in silence, and then she said, "It's my fault she was there. It should have been me."

Daniel watched her teeter on the edge of a snake hole of

misery. He tried pulling her back. "What was she like?"

Her eyes lit up. "She was the best big sister anyone could ask for. She taught me how to read. How to brush my hair. How to go potty." She laughed. "She was more like my mom than my mom. . . ." Her voice trailed off as she became lost in thought. Then she said, "I followed her everywhere. She was fearless and she was always looking out for me." Her eyes turned glassy. "I'd begged and begged and begged to go with my father on one of his work trips. Sometimes we were allowed to go. He'd been sick. It was nothing really, just a stuffy nose, but I was just a little kid, I thought the world was ending and I wanted to take care of him. But then I got sick too. My parents said I couldn't go on the trip. So I begged her to take my place, and I knew she had other things she'd rather be doing, but she said yes anyway. So she went. And she never came back."

The whole story seemed to make sense to Ionica, but for Daniel it was just bits and pieces, and there was a lot missing.

"What was her name?" he asked.

And just like that, the spell was broken. Ionica's eyes hardened. She'd said too much.

"I think that's enough talking for tonight," she said.

Baffled, Daniel held out his hands. "What did I say?"

Ionica lay on the blanket but would not respond. She watched the stars. A single tear trickled out and ran down toward her ear, but she said nothing and would not look at him.

Daniel lay down beside her but did not push. He felt like he should say something. Anything. Tell her he was glad they were friends and it was not her fault, but he didn't know how to say it without it sounding awkward or weird.

He studied the unfamiliar constellations, and after some time, fell asleep.

17

UNEXPECTED GUESTS

"Ionica! You have visitors!"

Ionica's mother sounded as though she were both far away and shouting right in his ear all at the same time. Daniel stirred.

Half asleep, he pried his eyes open to see someone standing over him.

"What the blazes is going on here?" a familiar voice asked.

"Ben? What are you doing here?"

Daniel yawned, looking around. They'd fallen asleep on the deck. But everything looked exactly the same as before. Twilight overhead. Darkness in one direction, a hint of dawn in the other. Exactly as it looked when he'd first arrived. "This is weird. . . ."

"No night and day here, remember?" Ionica rubbed her eyes.

"How do you get used to it?"

Ionica got up and shook her blanket out. "What time is it, anyway?"

"Time you two woke up," said Astrid from the doorway, holding a traditional stack of brightly colored Luminara presents.

Ionica bit her lip. "Oh, Astrid, you shouldn't have. I didn't get you anything."

"What?" Astrid said. "These aren't for you. These are for Daniel."

Baffled, Daniel said, "Why?"

"Why? In case we were being watched," Ben explained, incredulous. "We needed to get here without arousing suspicion."

"Who would expect a couple of kids loaded with presents to be up to no good on Luminara?" Astrid added brightly.

"I would. Have you met Dan?" said Ben.

"Why *are* you here?" Daniel persisted.

"I came up with a solution," Astrid explained. "About an hour after you two left Orpheus Core, I had this brain wave! Tor Torin said we could come and try it as long as Ben and I were safely back aboard the *Equinox* before the festivities begin. I'm afraid that's all the time we've got."

Daniel's heart soared. "Torin is here?"

"Of course. Now, is there somewhere we can do this?"

"Do *what*?" Ionica insisted.

"Remove Daniel's Identifier. You have six hours before you're expected to go out in public and attend the Luminara celebrations," Astrid said. "That's more than enough time for me to perform the procedure. You'll have one less thing to worry about, if you know that this mystery person isn't using Daniel's chip to track him."

"The garage," Ionica replied quickly. "We can lock everyone out. No one will know what we're up to."

Astrid nodded. "Good," she said. "Now, where's Jasper?"

Guilt seeped out of Daniel's pores. "Look, about that. I'm sorry. He just snuck aboard the Air-Drive."

Astrid sighed with relief. "It's about time he started following my instructions."

"What?"

"Let's just get to the garage," Astrid insisted.

They all followed Ionica down to the lower level and piled into a garage that appeared to double as Mimias Lux's workshop. There was a workbench and tools and gadgets of all kinds against the back wall. Mimias's Air-Drive sat gleaming under the harsh lights.

They ripped open the presents and pulled out all of Astrid's equipment that she'd smuggled in. When the miniature lab was fully set up, they found an old chair and had Daniel sit in it.

Astrid picked up a long thin metal probe. "Hold still," she ordered.

Daniel gripped the armrests. His knuckles turned white

while she coaxed the skin on the side of his head to peel back, revealing the socket underneath.

"What's the plan here?" said Daniel.

"I understand you're nervous, but you shouldn't feel a thing," Astrid said.

Daniel wasn't convinced. "Did you read that in a book?"

Astrid flashed a smile a little too quickly. "Yes! How did it sound?"

"Like you read it in a book," Daniel replied flatly.

Astrid brushed it off. "Well, medicine really isn't my thing. It said I had to rehearse something called a bedside manner."

"Just do what you're best at," Daniel said, looking to Ben for reassurance.

Ben shrugged, as if to say, *How am I supposed to know if it is going to hurt?*

Astrid swapped out her probe tool for one that lit up at one end and made an awful high-pitched whine.

"Is that the Transparent Officer?" Daniel asked.

"Transductive Oscillator!" she snapped. "Just be prepared. You might feel a slight vibration inside your skull," she explained, adjusting the setting and making the light flicker ever so faintly.

Daniel took a deep breath. Reaffirmed his grip on the armrests. "Let's get on with it," he said. If his knuckles turned any whiter, the bones would pop out.

Astrid eased the device up to the opening in Daniel's head.

"Wait!" Daniel objected.

Astrid flinched. "What's wrong?"

"Shouldn't we have an adult with us? A doctor or something? What if something goes wrong and you explode my brain?"

"You'd have to have a brain for it to explode," Ben quipped.

"We can always stop," Astrid said. "It's up to you."

Daniel took another breath as he chewed it over. "Okay," he said. "Let's go for it."

"You're sure?"

"No. But do it anyway."

Astrid gently squeezed the trigger.

Immediately Daniel's right leg twitched and jerked.

"Whoa, whoa!" Daniel cried, clinging desperately to the chair and trying not to get flung out of it. "What the heck was that?"

"I said, hold still," Astrid admonished.

"I *am* holding still. I didn't do that. *You* did!"

Astrid snatched the probe away in a whirl of curiosity and excitement. "A reflex response! How extraordinary! We knew this socket was wired into your central nervous system, but I think we just found the primary command path." She set the device down, suddenly almost afraid to use it anymore. "I'll need to make some more adjustments."

"What is it you're trying to do exactly?" Ionica stood to the side, her arms folded.

118

"Confuse the socket," Astrid explained. "Overload its inputs so that it will shut down. Because if we just remove the chip on its own, the socket knows that it's missing and starts attacking its host—in this case, Daniel. That's why his leg was jumping all over the place."

Astrid reset the oscillator and tried again. Daniel's leg quivered, kicking out to the side this time.

She reset the oscillator a third time and checked his vital signs on the monitor. "Okay, ready?"

Daniel's arms were getting tired from gripping the arm-rests, but what else was he going to do? "Sure," he said.

She gave his socket another jolt—

Daniel's leg shot up into the air, followed very quickly by Daniel himself, who backed up into a corner, intent on keeping his distance. "Okay," he said, "I think that's enough."

A wisp of smoke curled around his head.

He sniffed the air. "Do you smell something?" he said.

Ionica and Ben both eyed each other nervously. "Nope. Not a thing."

Click!

A tiny dark object sprang out of his socket and clattered to the floor. Daniel's Identifier. It was smoking.

Astrid scooped it up, turning the tiny black square over between her fingers. "This is a standard-size RC-808! I knew it!"

Daniel suddenly clutched his head with both hands.

"That's great," he said between gritted teeth.

Sharp, needling pains shot from one side of his brain to the other, bouncing around inside his skull like a ricocheting blaser bolt.

He dropped to his knees and screamed.

"Everything'll be fine," Astrid said quickly, rummaging around in her mobile lab.

"Everything is *not* fine!" Daniel protested.

Pain seared behind his eyeballs.

"Obviously this is not working," Ionica snapped. "Put it back in!"

"Not yet," Astrid protested, still searching.

Daniel shrieked.

"Astrid! It's going to kill him. Put the Identifier back! *NOW!*"

"Bloody hell, Astrid." Ben stormed over to swipe the tiny square chip from her hand.

Astrid moved faster. "Here!" she said, pulling a garish yellow chip from her mobile lab. "It's time we tried this." Aside from the color, it looked just like Daniel's Identifier chip.

She jammed it into a tiny rectangular device alongside the Identifier and watched the lights on the device pulse rapidly.

"Astrid!" Ionica demanded. "What are you doing?"

"Syncing the pathways!"

"What does that even mean?"

"Done!" Astrid declared. She grabbed the yellow chip and crouched down beside Daniel.

He rolled onto his side, his shocked body twitching and convulsing. He clawed at his head, but the pain wouldn't go away.

"Hold still," Astrid said.

"He can't hold still!" Ben cried.

"Then *you* hold him!"

Ben quickly grabbed Daniel by the shoulders and pressed down hard while Astrid struggled to get the yellow chip into the socket's command circuit. When she felt it click into place she let go and gestured for Ben to do the same.

Daniel's breathing began to slow. His head cleared. Within moments he lay sprawled on his back, still, staring up at the ceiling.

Everyone breathed easy. Ben licked his lips. "Are you okay, Dan?"

Daniel struggled to sit up. Astrid helped him. "What did you do?"

She grabbed his Identifier chip and showed him. "I swapped it out for a scrambler. The system thinks this chip is still in there. But if anyone tries to take control of you now—they're going to get very frustrated."

She handed his old Identifier back to him.

Daniel examined it while Astrid analyzed his head with a wide flat glass panel that seemed to show every conceivable thing hidden under his skin. The socket stood out as distinctly mechanical compared to the flesh and bone around it. It extended deep into his brain, where thin wires spread out like the arms of an octopus. Technical specifications blinked in and out of view as she homed in on what interested her the most.

"I'm not broadcasting my identity anymore?" Daniel asked, almost afraid of the answer.

"Nope," Astrid confirmed.

"Good," Daniel said. He tossed his old Identifier on the floor and, with a satisfied stomp, ground it to pieces under his heel.

"No!" Astrid shrieked, but it was too late.

Daniel didn't think he'd done anything wrong. "What?" he demanded.

"I was going to hook it up to Jasper! If that's how you're being monitored, we were going to use him as a decoy." She gritted her teeth. "That's why I sent him. You've ruined everything!"

18

THE LIGHT OF LUMINARA

That evening, long after they had said good-bye to Astrid and Ben, Daniel and Ionica made their way through the bustle of Traders Wharf.

Peoples mingled from thousands of worlds, eager to join the Luminara festivities. Daniel tried not to stare, not at the tall Sheckers with their white veils and silver bangles on their heads, or at the Guargum merchants, their callused fingers stained with dye.

Any one of them could be the messenger. Or not.

"I don't like this." Ionica glanced around, alert to every possible danger. "I don't like this at all."

Up ahead, her father raised his hand. "Everybody stay together," he warned. "It's very easy to get separated in a crowd of this size." He took his youngest son by the hand. "Is everyone excited?"

"Yeah!" Dimas cried, more elated than he probably should have been. "We're going to see a star blow up!"

Not quite the appropriate reaction.

"Do we stay with them?" Daniel asked. Now that his Identifier had been removed, did this mysterious messenger even know he was here? Hide in all the right places, Torin had said, and they will come to you.

"Let's break away when we reach the square," Ionica suggested.

"I agree." Daniel glanced back over his shoulder. Was he being followed yet? Hard to say. Even though he hadn't taken his eyes off the many faces in the crowd.

He hoped Tor Torin really was out here somewhere.

"Destination Square is that way," Ionica's mother insisted, following her husband into the crush of people milling around the side streets.

"Don't worry, we're taking a shortcut," Mimias explained.

"Well, I *do* worry. We'll miss it if we can't get in. Look at all these canopies over our heads. We won't see a thing."

The pungent smell of incense and Phracian spice wafted between the market stalls. Hawkers announced their bargains with chaotic cries. A rotund fellow in a long blue coat stood on a corner, ringing a holocule bell. Dhubbas walked side by side through the throng, singing hymns.

The shortcut turned out to be even more jam-packed than the main thoroughfares until, without warning, the way opened up to Destination Square; a wide-open plaza where hundreds of thousands of people had already gathered to witness the Festival of Light.

"There, see?" Mimias declared in triumph.

Around the entrance to the square, street vendors sold snacks and refreshments. The boys immediately wanted the sweetest, unhealthiest things they could lay their hands on, and now seemed like a good time to move on.

"Father," Ionica said abruptly, "I want to show Daniel around the square. He should get to see everything, since he's here for the first time."

Mimias Lux paused to think it over. "So long as you stay safe," he said.

Ionica rolled her eyes. "Father," she said. "We've been halfway across the galaxy and back. We're Truth Seekers. We can handle ourselves."

He nodded a halfhearted approval.

Giving her parents each a quick peck on the cheek, Ionica grabbed Daniel by the arm and steered him into the crowd.

Under the equator's permanent twilight, the festivities in Destination Square seemed to mirror the stars above, making it difficult to see where the crowd ended and the sky began.

When they reached a good distance from Ionica's family, near where a family played with holocule dust, creating oddball creatures for the children to play with, and where a Wag priest from Tularan stood meditating, Daniel let his true feelings out. "All this waiting around is driving me crazy."

"I just wish there was a better way," Ionica said.

And then, a familiar voice in the crowd. "How very thoughtful of me to give you the opportunity to be so generous!"

It sounded like Tor Torin.

Daniel craned his neck. It *was* Tor Torin! He was dressed like a street vendor, selling bags of roasted nuts. He doffed his cap on the way by and acted as if he'd never met them before today. "Happy Luminara," he said.

"Happy Luminara," the two Beacons responded.

Amid the crowd, more familiar faces began to reveal themselves. There was Raze Alioth! He looked uncomfortable out of uniform, pretending to be an ordinary reveler in an ugly sweater. And over there, Ionica's legendary skyriding mentor, Hella Phad!

The two friends let the relief wash over them.

"Thank God," Ionica said, with an anxious laugh.

It was short-lived relief. Within moments, Hella Phad, her elegant red hair swept back over her shoulders, began following a giant of a man who was heading toward them from the south. He shifted his large frame awkwardly as he squeezed between bystanders.

Daniel held his breath and tried not to stare. Was this the messenger? The gargantuan fellow drew closer and closer, until, before Daniel could think of what to do, the man had completely passed him by on his way to some other part of the square.

False alarm.

Hella Phad stopped following, and cut away through the crowd in another direction entirely.

It went on like that for an hour. Then two. Then three. Anyone who appeared to be coming in Daniel's direction picked up a shadow, only to lose it again when it became clear that they had no interest in him.

Until, that is, right around the time the crowd began to count down to the arrival of Earth's dying light, when Daniel became aware of a figure standing just off to one side, watching him.

This *had* to be the messenger.

The stranger had a slight, wiry build, and a scarf over his face. As he moved closer he would occasionally bump into people and make a great show of apologizing and wishing them a happy Luminara.

"He's here," Daniel said quietly to Ionica.

"FIVE!" the crowd roared.

Ionica craned her neck. "Where?" she asked.

"FOUR!"

"Just be ready," Daniel said.

"THREE!" the crowd cheered.

"You too," she replied, still not sure who Daniel was talking about. "All the lights will go out when they reach zero, to watch the flash in the sky."

"TWO!"

"Oh, I'm ready," Daniel said, determined to show who-ever this was that they no longer had the upper hand.

"ONE!"

Destination Square plunged into darkness. With all eyes on the night sky and the imminent flash of an exploding star, the messenger made his move.

Daniel sensed a hand reach out toward him. Even though his eyes hadn't yet adjusted, without warning, he spun on his heel and grabbed the messenger by the wrist. "Who are you?" Daniel demanded.

The messenger was not as surprised as Daniel had hoped. He twisted his arm and slipped out of the grip. Then in one bound, shot off into the crowd at a full tilt.

"No, Daniel! Wait!" Ionica yelled.

It was too late. Daniel was already chasing after him.

19

PURSUIT!

Daniel tore out of the square, not caring who he had to elbow out of the way to do it.

The messenger dodged in and out of the revelers. Leaping over arms and legs. For one glorious moment, Daniel actually gained on him—until *slam!*

He ran straight into the giant from earlier. Drote meat and hot chook spilled everywhere. The giant swung his arm. Daniel ducked. The giant grabbed at him but came up with a fistful of thin air.

Daniel ran and didn't look back.

He had to get him. Whoever he was—this messenger who had been messing with his mind. Why did this person know so much about him? About the ship. About the fact that he even went to the ship. What more did he know?

The messenger darted toward a side street before taking

an abrupt turn into a narrow gap between two storefronts. He leapt into the air, his feet skittering up the walls before he backflipped into the void beyond the handrail and plummeted down into—into where?

Daniel barreled over to the handrail. Whoever this was, they had planned this escape route. They knew that this narrow opening was here.

Below, the chaotic disks of the lower levels of Traders Wharf, bazaars, and auction spaces lined the canyon in interconnected stacks.

Where was this messenger? Where was he!

A massive beam called a yardarm extended out beyond the handrail, canopies lashed to it.

Whompff!

Daniel blasted out over the rail. Landed on the tip of the yardarm and listened.

He was down there somewhere, running in the dark.

All Daniel needed was—

Suddenly, the sky lit up with an enormous flash. The light of Luminara had arrived, and for one brief moment, the twilight city of Vespertine knew daylight.

There! There he was! Exposed for all to see.

Daniel swiped up his holographic display, jabbed a finger at the messenger, and said, "Track target!"

Bright holographic red crosshairs wrapped around the messenger.

Daniel was about to jump when a massive *whompff!* rocketed past his head.

Ionica landed on the roof of a building on the opposite side of the canyon.

Comms cut in.

"Where is he?" Ionica demanded. All business.

Daniel tapped the hologram, transmitting a copy of the target location straight to her. Then he jumped. Down two levels.

With another burst from his Aegis, he careened onto the walkway of the lower-level bazaar, narrowly missing a sprawling mass of glass-laden market stalls.

Already the light was starting to wane, the landscape fading back into the shadows.

The red crosshairs bobbed and weaved. The messenger was now half a mile away. He was so fast!

Another *whompff* exploded off in the distance. Hella Phad had joined the chase. She twisted. Turned. Landed on the first in a long line of canopies. Then ran across the fabric as though she were weightless.

Daniel darted on. Through alleyways. Over crates. Without pause. Leaping from bazaars on one side of the canyon to the other. Then back again.

Pain shot through Daniel's heels. He didn't care. If this messenger knew about the ship, maybe he knew about *him* and about who he really was! About who his family was!

The red crosshairs suddenly grew bigger. And bigger. Then dove down toward his feet. The messenger had jumped down to a lower level. And another.

He was running out of places to go.

Daniel knew just how to cut off his escape.

Ignoring the comms chatter between Ionica and the other Truth Seekers, Daniel launched himself into the dark. Rage propelled him.

He wanted to scream. To tear this messenger apart.

Where do I come from? Answer me!

Wrapping a ball of furious energy around his fist, Daniel punched at the air, smashing a hole through the floor of the platform below.

The messenger looked up. It was too late.

Daniel yanked him off his feet and the two of them plowed through the dirt like a meteor striking the ground.

Without wasting another moment, Daniel ripped the scarf from his face.

Correction.

Her face.

She was just a young girl. A terrified young girl. She couldn't possibly know anything about him, or his past.

But she'd been so fast. So strong.

Daniel shoved her roughly back into the dirt. "Who are you?" he roared.

"Daniel," a soothing voice gently commanded from somewhere behind him. "Daniel, let her go. It's all right."

Daniel refused. With tears in his eyes, he glared at Tor Torin. Beside the Keeper, Hella Phad stood with her hands on her hips. Raze Alioth landed a few paces away just moments later.

"Who is she?" Daniel demanded.

Ionica stood up from the deep trench in the ground that their impact had made. Clutching trinkets. Money. Gems.

"She's just a pickpocket," she said.

At first glance, Daniel refused to believe it, but with clearer eyes, it was hard to ignore the petty thief's haul spilling out of her ripped pockets.

"You're nobody," Daniel said, stunned.

The girl didn't dare speak.

"You're nobody!" Daniel raged, letting her go.

Torin laid a hand on Daniel's shoulder. "Nobody's nobody," he reminded him. "Look at the tattoo on her neck. She's from Insar. She's naturally far stronger and faster than most. Juba's a playground to her. She's probably part of a gang."

Daniel got to his feet. "I don't care about some gang."

"The people who were robbed probably do," Phad said.

"Once again, Mr. Coldstar, you display uncanny luck," Alioth mused. "Solving a crime no one knew was even being committed."

"Luck?" Daniel yelled. "What luck? I still don't know who sent me those messages. They may be long gone by now!"

"We don't know that," said Ionica.

"Daniel," Torin insisted, "we'll find another way."

"What other way?" Daniel raged.

He kicked up dirt as he walked away.

20

BEST-LAID PLANS

Daniel and Ionica hardly talked all the way back to her house.

He went straight to his room, the Lux family guest room, and lay in the dark feeling foolish and angry.

After a while, Ionica banged on the door and tried to come in, but he'd already locked it. "Dinner's ready," she said.

"I'm not hungry," he shot back.

"You're being a baby."

"I don't want to talk about it," he said.

"I don't want to talk about it either; I'm just doing what I'm told."

"By who?"

"My dad. He thinks you should eat something," she explained. "He thinks you'll feel better. I don't care if you starve."

He listened to the sound of her footsteps as she walked away.

He needed to be alone. Why didn't they understand that? An hour later, message alerts started bleeping on his scroll relentlessly. They went unanswered.

At midnight, another chime pulled him from his restless sleep.

Annoyed, Daniel refused to answer.

The scroll chimed again.

Daniel rolled onto his side and watched the little holographic message ball spin above the nightstand where his scroll sat, like some planet floating effortlessly in space.

"Go away," he whispered into his pillow. "Just leave me alone."

His scroll chimed a third time.

Irritated, Daniel leaned over to swipe the message away, but as he reached out, he noticed that the message wasn't from Ionica as he'd expected.

There was no name.

Daniel snatched the scroll off the table and opened up the hologram.

The message read: How did you enjoy Luminara?

Daniel's heart stopped.

It was him again. Or her. Or it. What if this whole time he'd been communicating with an artificial intelligence somewhere sitting on a computer?

Okay, be rational, Daniel thought. Half the people in the galaxy had just celebrated Luminara. Like Torin had said about the last message, this was vague enough that it felt personal, but it was just messing with his mind.

"I had a quiet time at home with the kids, you know, the usual," Daniel scoffed, amusing himself. He wasn't going to play this game. He swiped the message away and set his scroll back down where he'd found it.

A moment of silence in the darkness, and then another message bubble popped up with a ding.

Now this was getting on Daniel's nerves. He opened the message.

It read: It didn't look very quiet. Good work with that pickpocket.

What?

Daniel sat bolt upright in bed. He hadn't sent a reply. How did he or she know what he'd just said? Was his room bugged? Could they hear everything he was saying? And how did he know about the pickpocket unless—unless he was there?

What in blazes should he do?

Torin had to know right away, but how was he going to get a message to him without tipping this person off?

Paralyzed, Daniel sat in the darkness as another holographic sphere bubbled up.

This one read: Sorry about the distraction. I needed to know who was watching you. I can't have any other Truth Seekers involved. Not yet.

"Who are you?" Daniel asked aloud.

Another chime. Another message. You'll know soon enough, if you agree not to involve anyone else. For now.

Daniel's breath caught in his throat. How were they doing this? Why were they doing this?

"What do you want from me?" he demanded.

Your help, came the speedy reply.

A tinging, clattering kind of sound drew close to the side of the bed. Daniel peered down and, by the dim light of the holographic messages, found Jasper, terrified, his beak chattering like teeth.

"What is it?" Daniel urged. "What's wrong?"

Quaking in his webbed feet, the little anatom raised a flipper and aimed it at the darkness across the room.

A cold sweat seeped down Daniel's back. What was hiding in the dark?

There was only one way to find out.

"Lights! Full!" Daniel commanded.

The room filled with a blinding flash.

Someone was standing at the foot of his bed.

Cloaked in black rags, its face an emotionless mask with two deep-set holes for eyes. A Purgent, massive and silent.

Daniel threw himself back in his bed, a shiver running the length of his spine.

How long had it been there?

Despite legs of jelly, Daniel sprang to his feet, firing up his Aegis with a wave of his hand.

Whompff!

The room filled with the hum and howl of a whirling vortex.

The Purgent did not react. It calmly watched him, a towering pillar of menace, but it did not move.

"How did you get in here?" Daniel barely managed to say. His throat was tight and dry.

The Purgent said nothing. Could say nothing. It simply stood its ground.

"I can end you right now," Daniel warned.

The Purgent did not flinch. Instead, it gestured to a pile of black robes similar to its own that it had laid out on the bed.

Another message appeared on Daniel's scroll. For a moment he was torn. If he answered, would it attack? Daniel jumped down off the bed. Backed up to the nightstand, Jasper jammed behind his legs, his Aegis shield still spinning violently. He wasn't ready to let his guard down just yet.

Never taking his eyes off the Purgent, he reached over and tugged the scroll closer. He flicked at the holographic icon.

The final message read: The disguise is for you. Follow my Purgent. Alert no one or this will all be for naught. You have one hour or our meeting will never take place.

21

THE BOWELS OF TRADERS WHARF

Daniel followed the Purgent through the maze of Vespertine's markets.

The festivities had quieted down, but trade never stopped at Traders Wharf. Deals were struck, auction houses were alive with competing bidders, and fights were breaking out over slights and shoddy goods.

It was an odd feeling, being a Purgent for the night. People glared at him and cursed, or said things that were even more unrepeatable. Others would spit. A few simply got out of his way. All had that look of disgust on their faces.

It was enough for Daniel to want to take pity on the stoic figure leading him through the bazaar. How did he feel to be subject to all this, every waking moment? Here was a soul who had done unspeakable horrors, but who had committed to purging himself of those sins. He could not react, for he would lose his life. Was the suffering worth it?

But these thoughts were interrupted when Daniel realized where they were going.

The stench of raw sewage came first. It grew worse as they descended through narrow back alleys and even narrower staircases, beneath a canopy of leaking pipes, until they stepped down into the muddy underworld beneath the market stacks. Following the zigzagging trails that cut through a sea of garbage, past dimly lit reactors and treatment tanks, they came to a foul-looking reclamation plant where enginoids and anatoms stripped usable parts from discarded versions of similar robots and the like.

Daniel kept his distance when the Purgent stood by the open doorway to the plant and gestured for him to step inside.

Daniel wanted to ask what was in there, but there was no way to question the Purgent. He didn't know if Purgents could speak, or even if they were permitted to do so. Yet more troubling, he didn't know who else might be down here watching and waiting for his disguise to slip.

No light spilled out from inside the plant. There was just a dark void and a decision to make: turn around, or go in.

Daniel's stomach tightened into a knot. Yes, he had his Aegis and his uniform on under all this, and he had his training as a Truth Seeker. But that didn't mean he was in any way ready or protected.

Yet if he did not go inside, he'd never find out the truth.

Assuming there was a truth to find out. Besides, why would anyone use such an elaborate ploy to get him down here when there had been ample opportunity to ambush him during the celebrations earlier?

Perhaps it was naïve, but when Daniel made his decision, he didn't just walk inside the plant; he strode with confidence.

As he stepped into the darkness, he heard the Purgent follow him. A moment later, the door hammered shut with a *shooom-kathunk*. A series of small lights blinked on the door's control panel, turning red once the door had locked.

Now what? Were they just going to stand here in the dark?

Wait a minute. He didn't have his Identifier anymore. If this all went wrong, there would be no one coming to save him.

Was it too late to leave? How would he get out?

Plink. Plink. Plink.

One by one, panels of room lighting snapped on, revealing a dozen or so ragged Purgents waiting for them.

The first Purgent to reveal themselves was the one who had brought Daniel here. Reaching up, he eased his mask off and revealed his face: it was Ionica's father.

Aghast, Daniel stumbled back a step. This couldn't be real. How could this be real?

Mimias Lux turned to Daniel and said, "Is my daughter alive?"

22

SECRETS REVEALED

Daniel didn't know how to respond.

His mouth flapped open but nothing came out. He watched the other Purgents, but they remained motionless.

"Is my daughter alive?" Mimias asked again.

Confusion gripped Daniel by the throat and would not let go. Ionica was fine. "You know she is," he stuttered. "We were just at your house twenty minutes ago. Is she in danger?"

"No. Not that daughter," Mimias snapped. "My *other* daughter."

Nothing Mimias was saying made sense to Daniel.

"Take the disguise off," Mimias ordered. "We're safe here. All clear," he announced to the others.

Safe? Was that some kind of joke?

Daniel watched the Purgents begin pulling off their

masks, revealing adults underneath, men and women from various worlds, age and worry etched on their faces.

"This is the boy?" one woman said. Her eyes were like violet gemstones, her skin cracked in a thousand places like fish scales.

Who were these people?

Daniel's hands shook. He eased the mask from his face and tried not to drop it. "I don't know your other daughter," Daniel protested. "I don't even know her name."

"Son, the last time I saw her alive," Mimias pressed, "she was with *you*."

"That's not possible!"

Mimias ignored him and pulled a round, pewter-colored imager from a pouch. He held it in the palm of his hand and activated it. A hologram flickered into the air, showing a picture of Mimias with his arm around his daughter, on board a starliner in happier times.

Not Ionica—a different girl. One who Daniel recognized instantly.

"Nova . . . ?" he whispered in shock.

"I told you you knew her."

The girl who had risked everything to sneak him food when he'd been imprisoned in the pit back in the relic mines. The first girl he had any memory of ever meeting. "She said she knew me. But I didn't know her." The room began to spin. "Where is this?" Daniel said, his voice growing thin and weak.

"You know where this is," Mimias replied. "You were

there." Mimias clenched his teeth and fiddled with the imager. The picture zoomed in to reveal Daniel, younger but still obviously him, standing over Nova's shoulder, some distance away, watching whoever was taking the picture.

"Is this aboard the *Coldstar*?" Daniel asked. "*You* sent me the map?"

Mimias spoke, but Daniel couldn't hear him; his thoughts and emotions whirled, threatening to turn him inside out. What in all the galaxy was going on here? "Ionica said Nova died."

"Ionica doesn't know what she's talking about."

"I don't remember this picture. I saw Nova in the mines," Daniel explained desperately. "But that was a long time ago."

Besides, how was he supposed to explain that the last he time he saw Nova she had been turned into a mindless foot soldier in the Mythrian Army?

"But you *saw* her!"

"Yes."

Mimias nodded, choking back emotion, as though he'd just made up his mind about something. "That's all I needed to hear. I haven't heard anything in over two years."

Daniel's eyes darted around the room as he tried to put the pieces together. "If I was there, then that must mean my parents were there too. Right?"

Ionica's father shook his head. "If they were there, I didn't meet them. I'm sorry."

Tears welled in Daniel's eyes. They spilled down his

cheeks but he refused to acknowledge them. Refused to sob. "Why did the Sinja take me?" Daniel begged.

Mimias paused. He looked down at Daniel as though seeing him for the first time. The tension across his face seeped away. He patted Daniel on the shoulder and clutched the back of his neck. "Oh, son," he said. "I'm so sorry. I keep forgetting you're just a kid. This is a vicious game."

"What game?" Daniel prodded.

"The game of power." Mimias looked to the other adults dotted around the room. When he turned back to Daniel he said, "Do you know what it is I do?"

Daniel vaguely remembered Mimias mentioning something at dinner that first night. "You work for the Juban Defense Directorate," he said.

"Do you know *why* I work for the Defense Directorate?" Daniel shook his head. "No."

"Because the Sinja *demanded* it of me," he explained, his voice cold. "Kijka, tell him what you do."

A man with a nose like a raptor's beak and eyebrows that showed no hint of a curve gave Daniel a grave look from across the room. "I work at the Mandaradan shipyards. The Sinja have me steal blueprints of War Guild ships so that they know their weaknesses. They say I have no choice if I want to see my son alive again."

The man named Kijka fished out his own imager and called up the hologram of a young boy, his hair slicked back. "His name is Haru." His voice cracked. "Have you seen him? Was he in the mines with you?"

Daniel didn't recognize the boy. "I'm sorry," he said.

"Please look again," the man insisted.

"I'm sorry. *Really.* I don't know him. I haven't seen him," Daniel explained, feeling acid sloshing around inside his gut.

Mimias gestured to one of the women to speak. "Tell him your story, Deminae."

The woman with the fish-scale skin went to speak, but Daniel didn't want to hear any more stories. Horrified, he backed away, his head filled with the terrible echoes of the Nightwatchers in the mines, forever burned into his memory.

Who disturbs . . .

Who disturbs . . .

Was that why the grubs were chosen each night to be disappeared? Not because they had done something wrong, but because their parents had displeased the Sinja in some unimaginable way? But if that were the case, why had Daniel been taken and then returned? Had his parents redeemed themselves in the eyes of the Sinja?

What had they done?

"We're bargaining chips?"

"Yes."

"That's *it*?"

"Isn't that enough?" Mimias said. "They took our children and still hold them hostage. They could have chosen wicked men to do their bidding. Men who could be bought and whose morals change with the weather. But they didn't. They chose good men. And how do you make a *good* man

do a wicked thing? You take what he holds most precious—
and threaten to take her away forever."

He rubbed his hands and patted his legs, trying to find
the right words.

"I didn't always work for the Defense Directorate," he
said. "I'm a scientist. A professor. I was invited to present
my research to fellow scientists aboard that *starliner.*" Mimias all but spat the last word out. He took a breath. "When
the Sinja came, I gave them what they asked for. Anything
to save my little girl. It wasn't enough. They took my
research, and then took her anyway," Mimias explained.
"Then they crashed the ship, to hide their evil so we could
explain to our families why our children were gone."

Mimias glanced at his feet, shame washing over him.

"A few months later they made more demands of me. So
I did what they asked, to save Nova. And they asked again.
And again. Each request more horrifying than the last. And
each time they refused to uphold their end of the bargain.
They refused to let her go." He looked Daniel right in the
eye. "But what could I do to keep her alive? We are *all* good
people in this room, Daniel Coldstar. But every one of us
here has a life depending on us."

Daniel gasped, hunched forward, clutching his knees. He
needed air! He needed air, now! Why couldn't he breathe?

This is why he was taken? This was why the Guild of
Truth could never find any evidence of so many missing
children across the galaxy, because their parents were too
afraid to say anything?

Another woman stepped forward, her eyes a striking blue. "This is all just a vast web," she said, "stretching from one side of the galaxy to the other. And we're all just bugs caught in it. You think the Tarafand and Oota Mheen simply went to war because propaganda told them to? Look closer. Look deeper. Who made decisions against their own interests? Who compromised their worlds in ways that made no logical sense? Ask yourself what the Sinja had over them, and you will find your answer."

Daniel stood frozen while he watched. The closer she drew, the more familiar she seemed. What amazed him the most were her eyes, her searing blue eyes—with no sign of a pupil.

"Are you from the Burn Worlds?" he said.

She nodded. "Kith," she said.

"Who did the Sinja take from you?" he asked, afraid of the answer.

"You think you know Kardas?" she asked, sounding hopeful.

Daniel had never heard the name Kardas before in his life. Somehow he didn't think it mattered.

"May I see him?"

The woman nodded and lit up her imager. A boy's face shimmered into existence.

Daniel knew him all right, but under a different name.

"Blink," he said.

23

SHADOW OF THE SINJA

"Why do you look afraid?" the woman asked.

Daniel eyed Mimias but he was no help. Daniel was on his own.

"What's wrong?" she asked, panic creeping into her voice. "You called him Blink. That's his nickname. Is that the name he goes by–?" Her voice caught in her throat. "Is that the name he *went* by? Is my son dead?"

"No!" Daniel replied, afraid of the things he knew he was going to have to tell her. "He was my friend."

She trembled. She didn't seem to know what to do with herself. She inched toward him but he inched farther back.

"My first memory of him," he said, hoping she would stop, "was when he ran in to save me from a beating. . . ."

He could see it all in his mind's eye even now. The Racks. The Overseers with their blast-pikes ready to strike.

Who disturbs . . .

Who disturbs . . .

Blink's mother looked ready to crumple. "He helped you?" she said.

Daniel nodded.

"We called him Blink, because that's what he did," Blink's mother explained. Her chest heaved, caught somewhere between a sob and a laugh. "He always would run in without blinking. Always wanting to help. He was fearless."

"He was with me when we escaped," Daniel said. A dark cloud drifted across his brow. "Almost until the end." He didn't want to go any further.

"Tell me what happened," she urged. She didn't seem afraid, more relieved that she would finally get an answer.

She wouldn't like it.

Daniel tripped over his words, but he forced them out anyway. "Blink pledged himself to the Sinja," he said. "He became a follower of Vega Virrus."

She didn't believe him. She actually smiled. "That's not possible," she said.

Mimias held up a hand; meant to calm her, it only seemed to inflame her. "Laleh, please."

"It's impossible, I said!" The smile faded and the rage rushed in. "Kardas would not do that!"

Daniel gulped, but he stood firm. "It's what happened," he said.

Before he could step back again, Blink's mother shot forward and gently held his hands. "Kardas is a boy who cares deeply about everyone and everything around him. He has always been that way. When he was seven years old, there was a sand fire that swept through our property. We kept Keff lizards in a coop for the eggs and he ran in to save them before anyone could stop him. Lizards! The stupid boy." Sniffing back tears, she said, "You must believe me. If he did what you say—he did it for a reason. He probably thought he could help someone, and now he's trapped and he cannot get out."

Mimias laid his hand on her shoulder. "Laleh, come on now." He eased her away.

She shook him off, yelling, "He's not lost! He would not betray us! Think about it! Why would he do this?"

Daniel's mind raced. Was it possible that Blink hadn't joined the Sinja, but had infiltrated them instead? Why? To save the other grubs?

That's not how Blink had acted the last time he saw him.

Daniel tore at his scalp, but try as he might, he couldn't rip the confusion out. First Nova, now Blink.

Mimias turned back to Daniel. "In the scheme of things, all that matters is that together, all of us here, we can stop the Sinja before their plans go any further."

"How?" Daniel said. "There were thousands of us in the mines. Every planet in the galaxy must have some parent being manipulated by the Sinja."

A ripple of unrest spread throughout the assembled strangers. Thousands seemed like a far bigger number than they had been expecting.

Daniel couldn't believe it. "What, did you think you were the only ones?"

"It doesn't matter," Mimias said, trying to calm them. "It doesn't matter. We made the decision to do this, we go ahead with it."

"The decision to do what?" Daniel pleaded. "I don't know how to help you. I don't know what I'm supposed to do!"

"Son," Mimias reassured him with something resembling a smile, "we didn't call you here so you could help *us*. We called so we could help *you*."

He held out his imager again, urging Daniel to take it.

"This device isn't as it seems," he said. "I buried a private communications node in its workings. Get this to the Guild of Truth. We'll all be able to communicate without the Sinja ever knowing."

Daniel examined it with his fingers. "What are you planning?"

"Defiance," Mimias said. "We all found each other, and we will find others. We cannot openly resist the Sinja. Everyone in this room would be dead. But we can inform the Guild of Truth. If they know what to expect, they can thwart them at every turn."

"I understand."

"No, not fully you don't," Mimias corrected. "This imager also contains everything you need to know about our children, so that you can find them. Our confessions, should this all go wrong. And lastly—and this is *the* most important part of all, Daniel. I need you to understand— this device contains all of my research outlining *exactly* what it is the Sinja are searching for and what it is they hope to accomplish. The plan of the Achorint depends on the *Twelve*."

What did that mean? Daniel had no idea, but a chill wrapped itself tightly around his spine, pressing icy fingers deep into his bones anyway. He clutched the imager tightly before tucking it away into his utility belt, hidden under his Purgent robes.

"I promise," he said. "I promise that I'll get this to—"

An alarm sounded. Tiny but distinctive.

Mimias checked the notifier on his wrist. The color drained from his face. "They're here," he said.

Terror swept through the room.

"They're in orbit," Mimias added. "They came early. My God, they came early."

"*Who* are here?" Daniel demanded.

"The Sinja," Mimias snapped. "I *am* about to betray my entire world to try to save my child." He looked Daniel right in the eye. "Within the day, they are going to instruct me to lower Juba's defenses so that they can invade. Or they will kill Nova. I have no reason not to believe them. Get this information to the Guild of Truth, Daniel. *Run!*"

24

THE SINJA STRIKE!

Daniel ran!

Faster than he had ever run in his life. No time for rest. No time for anything. He had to get to Tor Torin at all costs.

"I don't understand," Ionica kept saying, yawning on the comms. "It's like six in the morning. Can't it wait?"

"No, it can't wait!" Daniel said, dumping the Purgent disguise on one of the piles of trash and bounding up the steps to the higher levels. "Find Keeper Torin. Make sure he's there. Guardian Phad. Guardian Alioth. Everyone!"

"Make sure he's where, exactly?"

"The Truth Consulate in Vespertine. Hurry, this is an emergency!"

"What–"

"And make sure you're there too!"

Daniel cut the channel and bounded up to the next level of the bazaar. Shocked passersby and traders quickly got out of his way, completely unprepared to see a Truth Seeker in full shining armor among them. It was nothing like when he'd passed through here as a Purgent earlier.

When he reached a stall with a gnarly faced old man, he shook his finger at him. "And *you* ever spit on a Purgent again, you'll have me to answer to. Got it?"

The old market trader stared, dumbfounded.

At a pier extending out over the canyon, Daniel waved a gold coin at a Bullet Courier. He wasn't sure of its value or even which currency it was supposed to be; Truth Seekers were always advised to keep something of value with them in their belt to trade in case of a situation. At least it seemed to make the rider's eyes light up. In a heartbeat he was hanging on to the back of the single-engine Bullet, careening between market towers and flying low over the sprawl of Traders Wharf, heading for downtown Vespertine.

When he jumped down onto the steps of the Truth Consulate, he glanced up at the sky. Ships were fleeing in massive numbers.

Inside the consulate, Truth Seekers were already hurrying to and from their stations. Comms channels blasted out security warnings from Juba's Defense Directorate.

>GLOBAL ALERT! GLOBAL ALERT!<

"What is going on?" Ionica demanded, rushing in

through one of the other entrances, Jasper trying to keep up behind her.

A busy Truth Seeker looked up. Grim. "Sinja warships, inbound for Juba," he said.

"What!"

"Come on," Daniel urged. "This is going to get a whole lot worse."

"How?" she asked, baffled, following his lead up to the top floor.

"Just don't hate me," he said.

Tor Torin and an entire council of Truth Seeker elders were gathered when the two of them arrived.

"What do you mean, they came out of nowhere?" Torin could be heard saying. "Surely you have an early-warning system?"

"The system is offline. We don't know how," the life-size holocule of the Juban Secretary of Defense explained. "Don't worry, the planetary defense grid *is* operational. But we *will* need reinforcements. It won't last forever."

"We've already petitioned the War Guild to send a front-line defensive blockade on your behalf, but I will be honest, Mr. Secretary. I do not believe they can get here in time," Torin confided. "If any of your allies owe you favors, now would be the time to call upon them."

The Juban Secretary of Defense nodded and fizzled out of existence.

Torin clutched his brow. "Finally, the Sinja make their

move. I just wish I understood it."

"*I* understand it," Daniel announced, drawing everyone's attention.

"Not now, Daniel," Guardian Alioth admonished. "This is serious."

"I'm being serious," Daniel fired back. He held up Mimias Lux's imager. "All the Sinja plans are contained on this."

Torin's mood darkened. "Where did you get that?"

"Mimias Lux gave it to me."

"My father? I've never heard anything so absurd," Ionica scoffed.

"*He's* the one who sent me the map to the *Coldstar*," Daniel explained. "And he's the one who lowered Juba's defenses."

Not a Truth Seeker in the room could ignore Daniel now. Alioth turned to Torin. "Why would he do that?"

"Daniel . . . ," said Torin, addressing him cautiously, as though he were trying to back a wild animal into a corner. "What's going on?"

Daniel didn't know how to say this without destroying Ionica, but time was not on their side. "Ionica's father is being blackmailed by the Sinja," he said.

"I don't believe it!" Ionica roared. "Why are you saying this?"

"Ionica, please calm down," Torin begged.

"How?" Hella Phad interjected. "How is he being blackmailed?"

Daniel never got a chance to answer.

Suddenly, every hologram imager in the room burst into life, each one displaying the same scene, over and over again; under a blinding sun, ancient ruins on a barren landscape, surrounded by rivers of oozing blue lava.

"What is this? What's going on?" Torin demanded.

Phad recognized the type of structure almost immediately. "That's a Destronomer temple," she said. "I didn't realize there was one on Juba."

Alioth glanced up from one of the consoles around the edge of the room. "We're locked out. I can't shut the imagers off."

"Is this a recording?" asked Torin.

Alioth shook his head. "This is happening right now."

"I want to know *where* this is happening," Torin declared.

Phad redirected their attention. "Someone's coming out," she said.

All eyes settled on the holograms; a band of oily Overseers were emerging.

When they reached their destination, they fanned out, revealing three Mythrian soldiers, their ancient armor buffed and gleaming. Two of them grabbed the third and marched him to the middle of the half circle, forcing him to his knees.

"How did they get down to the surface of Juba with no one noticing?" Torin wondered. "They have weapons. Armor. There's no way they could have smuggled them through the security grid."

In unison, the two Mythrian soldiers raised their weapons, aiming them squarely at their comrade.

"Helmet off," one of them commanded. "Hands on your head."

The soldier did as commanded, revealing a girl a few years older than Daniel and Ionica, her expression blank and emotionless. A long snakelike tether extended out from the helmet, plugging directly into the socket in the side of her head.

"What are they doing? Who is that?" Ionica said, her focus causing her to miss what was happening in the background. A man was emerging from the Destronomer ruins, his ragged cloak separated in the wind, forcing the long strips of black fabric to rise up behind him like tentacles. A dark Sinja with a face of blades, Vega Virrus, creator of the Mythrian Army, had arrived.

He took his place behind the kneeling girl.

"Mimias Lux," Vega Virrus whispered, "you should not have brought the Truth Seekers into this. Let the galaxy see you for who you truly are: a traitor to your people. Now, you will lower Juba's last remaining security grid and allow our ships to land. Or Nova Lux will die."

25

SISTERHOOD IS POWERFUL

"That is not my sister," Ionica protested adamantly. Her face contorted as though she had just ripped open an old wound, yet she refused to acknowledge the agony. "My sister is dead," Ionica said. "What kind of sick trick is this?"

"It's not a trick," Daniel explained. "It's really her."

"How would you know?" she snapped.

Daniel gulped. There was no way to sugarcoat this one; he'd just have to come right out and say it. "Because she looks exactly how she did the last time I saw her. In the relic mines."

Daniel watched Ionica, watched his betrayal slide across her face. She knew he was telling the truth.

She looked confused. Sickened. Distraught. Ionica backed up against the wall. "Why didn't you tell me?" she said.

"I *am* telling you. Right now," Daniel insisted. "I didn't know before today."

"You didn't know?" she raged. "We look so much alike, how could you not have made the connection before today?"

It was a reasonable question, but he didn't have a reasonable answer. "I don't know," he said, helpless. "I didn't think. So much has happened."

"You have too many secrets, Daniel Coldstar!" she roared. "Too many! What else aren't you telling me? What other surprises do you have up your sleeve?"

Daniel had never seen her like this. The red-faced fury. The tears. The disgust. For the first time since he had known her, he was afraid.

She jabbed a finger at one of the holograms. "I know where that is," she declared.

"Ionica," Torin said calmly. "Let's not do anything rash."

"Those are the Azul Flats," she said. "Now I'm going to save my sister, and none of you better think about trying to stop me."

And with that, Ionica Lux stormed out, leaving everyone to deal with the effects of such a hurricane.

Everyone knew that her chances of surviving such an encounter were close to zero.

Daniel ran for the door.

"Where are you going?" Torin demanded.

"To try and stop her," Daniel shot back, tossing him Mimias Lux's imager.

"You don't know this planet. You need protection!"

"There's no time!"

And with that, Daniel was out the door, leaving Torin and the other Truth Seekers to the chaos.

Outside, Ionica was already plugging into the old red Clodhopper that she had piloted here from her house.

He was never going to make it. The engine was already in gear and the legs were starting to retract as it flew away.

Without thinking, Daniel activated his Aegis.

Whompff!

Giving it everything he had without going splat on the side of a building, Daniel blasted himself at the vehicle, smacking into its rear end and hanging on to whatever he could grip as Ionica hit the accelerator.

He heard a tuneless hum of disapproval and looked up to find Jasper peering down at him.

"How did you get ahead of me?" Daniel cried.

Jasper dismissed him, tilting his head as if to say: *Really? That's a serious question?*

"Help me up," Daniel ordered.

The anatom didn't think so. He turned away in disgust and made himself comfortable in the backseat.

Great.

Gritting his teeth, his legs flailing, Daniel pulled himself up with all his might until he managed to tuck his whole body into the low-pressure zone directly behind the tail end of the vehicle and take a rest for a moment on the empty rear loading board.

Daniel brought up his comms and pinged Ionica.

"Go away," she said.

"Don't do this," he urged. "You'll get yourself killed."

"They'll never see me coming," she retorted.

"I hope not. One shot and this entire vehicle turns into a fireball!" Daniel yelled, trying to make himself heard over the rush of air.

"Dammit," Ionica said, talking to herself. "Is that traitor on my hopper?"

"I'm trying to stop you from making a mistake!"

"Get off before I throw you off."

"Look, I'm sorry!" Daniel said.

"Oh good! That makes it *all* better!" she snapped back.

Suddenly the vehicle spun into a barrel roll. Daniel cartwheeled, his feet barely skimming over the roof of a building, while his fingers struggled to keep him from falling.

"Will you stop that?"

"No," Ionica replied firmly, snapping the comms channel off.

When the Clodhopper righted itself, Daniel wasted no time climbing up over the back end and throwing himself through a window and into the seat beside her.

Quickly, he plugged himself in before she tried any more tricks.

Ionica wept openly, hunched over the steering column,

her jaw set. Nothing in the world was going to stop her.

"At least let me help," Daniel said.

"You've helped enough."

She hit the accelerator, forcing Daniel back into his worn leather seat.

The Clodhopper rocketed over the suburbs of Vespertine and into the parched, barren landscape of Juba's ferocious dayside. When the sun hit the windshield, it tinted automatically before they were both blinded. Hot air seared the compartment.

Daniel surveyed the rocky landscape far below. "Why did they come here?" he asked. "It's the middle of nowhere. Why stage something like this here?"

The great legend of the Mythrian Army, one that no one had ever seen in action yet, was that they could supposedly see the future and react accordingly. No one should be able to ambush them or trick them. That was why they were feared and why the Sinja had been so bent on their resurrection.

Unless—was that a lie?

A bleep followed by a warning light activated on the dash.

"We're in range of the temple," Ionica said.

"Good," Daniel replied, scouting for somewhere to land. "I'd start our descent before we get shot out of the sky."

"Let me know how you do," Ionica said, unplugging from the Clodhopper. "Better yet. Learn to skyride."

And with that she leapt out of the window and streaked across the sky with a terrific sonic *boom!* Which meant no one was flying the vehicle.

Daniel panicked. He reached for the wheel and hammered at the controls, but he was locked out.

"Ionica!" he screamed.

Up ahead, the Sinja ground forces had spotted him and were opening fire.

In the backseat, Jasper squealed in terror.

"Oh, now you want my help," Daniel said, tucking the anatom under his arm.

He kicked the hatch open.

They had no choice but to bail.

26

AZUL FLATS

Daniel plummeted.

How was he going to survive a fall from this altitude, Aegis or not? Ionica was a skyrider. This is what she did, what she trained for—Daniel had *none* of those skills!

KA-BOOOOOOM!!!

The Clodhopper exploded just a few miles away, its carcass a tumbling fireball streaking toward the ground.

Daniel looked away. He had bigger problems. The blue rivers of lava that snaked across the landscape were getting bigger and bigger. Perilous clouds of toxic gases burned his eyes and his throat.

He had to make a decision. Pick a spot to try to land on and hope he had enough control over his descent to make it—or die.

Whompff!

Daniel fired up his Aegis, blasting the air beneath him. Holy smokes! He hit the shock wave and bounded forward. His angle was shallower now. If he kept doing this, he might be able to hit the ground running, if he didn't come in too fast and break his legs.

Whompff!

Another shock wave beneath his feet. Not as strong as before. It felt strangely solid. There was nothing to see except the blast of superheated air, but for a brief moment it was solid enough for him to run two or three steps before it dissipated and he was tumbling again, his legs still pumping.

He tried again.

Whompff!

And again.

Whompff!

Then another. And another!

Whompff! Whompff! Whompff!

He was doing it! *This* was how skyriders ran through the air, by creating temporary pathways of small shock waves strung together. The key was to keep moving and never use too much power—

KA-BLAM!

Daniel blasted sideways as the air all around him ignited in a monstrous fireball. Jasper rocketed out of his arms and disappeared into the smoke while Daniel hit the ground hard, sliding on his back across the dirt and straight for the heat haze of oozing lava.

Panicked, Daniel instinctively threw up his arms.

Whompff!

A shock wave blasted out in front of him, igniting more of the noxious vapors and driving an invisible wedge into the stream of molten rock.

Lava spewed into the air like ocean waves crashing on rocks. Smoking chunks of lava hit the ground all around him.

Trapped, Daniel threw up a cocoon of pure energy and watched helplessly as boulder after boulder struck his shield, and blue lava slicked up over one side.

Daniel waited, afraid to move, long after hot rocks had stopped falling from the sky and the river of lava had returned to its normal course. He wanted to be sure there were no more surprises.

He watched the lava that had slicked up over one side of his shield cool, harden, and turn dark gray.

Was this all going to collapse on him the moment he lowered his shield?

Only one way to find out. Bracing for more trouble, he let his shield down.

He was met with the sound of cracking and then—

Nothing. Just the rotten stench of sulfur and the sound of bubbling.

The structure held.

He allowed himself to exhale.

He was alive.

And he hurt.

"Ouch . . . ," Daniel croaked.

He rolled over onto his knees and crawled out from under the curved pumice, looking like a trabasaur emerging from an egg.

"Jasper?" he called out. "Jasper!"

There was no reply.

He sure hoped the little anatom hadn't fallen in and met a grisly demise.

He staggered out into the open and attempted to get his bearings—

Hissssssssssssss!

A gigantic snakerd slithered up onto the newly formed rocky overhang. Its head was as big as Daniel's. It bared its fangs. Spread out its scaly wings—

And flew at him!

Daniel projected a whirling shield on his wrist, arced his arm through the air, and chopped the flying snake's head clean off.

It rolled to the ground, dead. Its body was still wriggling as its orange blood seeped into the dust.

Daniel bent over to catch his breath.

Forget the Sinja, this entire planet was going to kill him before they did.

Where the heck was he?

A thin column of black smoke spiraled up on the horizon. No doubt the Overseers were already checking the wreckage of Ionica's Clodhopper, hunting for survivors.

The position of the smoke also meant that the temple must be in that direction. And so was Nova. He just hoped Ionica had landed safely and hadn't been blasted out of the sky too.

Sweat beaded across his brow and down his neck. It had to be over a hundred degrees on the dayside of Juba. He wiped his face, smearing black soot over his sore hands. He was going to cook in this place.

Sliding his hand through the air, he pulled up his vital signs that were being monitored by his sleeks–his Truth Seeker uniform. The readings told him what he already knew: he wasn't going to survive in this heat with his uniform in its current configuration. He set the controls to cooling mode.

Immediately, the tiny metallic hexagons that made up his sleeks rearranged themselves, transforming from a kilt and tunic into a bodysuit. The hexagons slid down his legs, forming pants, while above his shoulders they rose up around his neck and over his head to form a hood.

It wasn't perfect, but it would make him a little more comfortable for his journey ahead.

Picking his way over the rocks, Daniel began the task of trying to find ways across the smaller rivulets and streams of lava without using his Aegis. He didn't want another cloud of fumes literally blowing up in his face.

"Jasper?" he cried more than once, but no response came back.

Daniel walked for what felt like miles, hopping and jumping over obstacles. He could see the Destronomer ruins in the distance now. He hesitated to call it a temple. It was likely that nobody really knew what it had been used for. If there was one thing he'd learned in his archaeology classes, it was that any time anyone didn't understand an ancient site, they classified it as ritual or religious.

Where was Ionica? He only hoped she hadn't run in to fight the Sinja on her own.

Reaching into his utility belt, he pulled out his trinoculars and scanned the horizon.

There. About a mile away, Ionica was kneeling down behind the lip of a sand bank, lava flowing all around her, talking to herself.

He thumbed the augment button. The trinoculars collected what sound they could pick up and boosted it. She was talking into her comms. It was faint, but he could distinctly hear her plea, "Father, answer me! Why did you lie to me?"

27

OUTFLANKING THE ENEMY

"We don't have much time," Daniel said, approaching Ionica from an angle where she could see him. The last thing he needed was her lashing out, thinking she was being ambushed.

Ionica ignored him, wiping her nose on the back of her hand.

"What, are you just going to sit there and feel sorry for yourself?" he prodded.

Ionica closed her eyes, as though shutting out the annoyance.

A knot formed in his stomach. "You come all this way and you're just going to give up?" The knot pulled tighter. He watched the muscles in her jaw clench. "Get up," Daniel urged.

Nothing.

"Get up!" he roared.

In one almighty bound, Ionica shot into the air and landed right in Daniel's face. "Don't. Tell me. What. To do."

Daniel tried not to flinch.

"You suddenly want to walk in there and take on the Sinja?" she growled. "You didn't even want to come."

"Well, we're here now," Daniel replied evenly. "So we may as well deal with it."

"And how do we deal with kids just like us? Kill them? It'd be like killing ourselves."

"Who says we have to kill anybody?" Daniel countered.

"This is *war*. That's what happens."

"That's what the Sinja want. That's what they do, but it doesn't have to be that way," Daniel insisted. "Not unless we let it. We're here for Nova. So let's get her and go."

"How?" Ionica responded, incredulous.

Daniel couldn't believe it. "I thought you had a plan?"

"I don't have a plan."

"Then what were you going to do?"

"I don't know! Do you have any ideas?"

Daniel started walking. "No," he said, waving his hands at the air. "We'll have to figure it out."

"Mmmm-hmmm-hmmmm."

Jasper waddled up over a dune, using his flippers to keep his balance. He picked his way down to join them.

"Jasper! Glad you're still in one piece," Daniel noted.

The anatom made a kind of farting noise but kept going.

The three of them edged closer to the ruins and the Sinja forces. Patrols roamed everywhere, searching for any survivors they had seen jump from the crashed vehicle.

Ducking down behind an eroded limestone ridge, Daniel stuck his trinoculars up on the overlook and sat back down, pulling up its readings on his holographic display.

The Destronomer ruins were expansive, most of them the remains of walls and other buildings covering a large area. At the center of the complex was the area everyone called the temple. The building stood several stories high and consisted of an immense ridged dome with entrances at the cardinal points. For such an ancient structure, it appeared completely intact and untroubled by age.

Virrus was nowhere to be seen, but twenty or so Overseers stood in front of the temple with their weapons still aimed at Nova. The Mythrian soldiers who had brought Nova to the forefront for the message to Mimias had reverted to patrolling the ruins. There weren't any ships.

"I don't understand how they got here," Ionica whispered. "What did they do, walk?"

Daniel had other questions. "If you could see the future, why would you need to go on patrol?" he whispered back. "Wouldn't you *know* the enemy was sitting out here watching you?"

They eyed each other. Had the Sinja's precious Mythrian Army turned out to be a dud?

From the interior of the temple an almighty *thrummmm* caused every atom around them to vibrate momentarily.

Now that had Ionica's attention. "What's going on in there? We *have* to find out," she whispered back.

"What about your sister?"

Clearly, in Ionica's mind this wasn't an either-or situation. "We get her too," she said.

Drawing her finger in the dirt, she outlined the temple and marked where the majority of the soldiers were standing with little *X*s.

"If we go in through here," she explained, as quietly as she could, "through the entrance out back, it'll give us enough cover to sneak up on them from behind."

Daniel balked. "Assuming there's nothing inside there that's going to want to kill us. I don't see Vega Virrus anywhere out here, do you? Maybe he's inside waiting."

The hairs on the back of Daniel's neck stood on end. He could feel Virrus's presence. Knew that he was here somewhere. It was only a matter of time before he stepped back out of the shadows.

"Isn't that the point?" Ionica whispered. "You were the one who told me to quit whining."

"That's not exactly what I said."

"You got a better idea?"

"No."

"Then let's go."

28

THE CHAMBER OF INFINITE DOORWAYS

Daniel and Ionica hunkered down, backs against the wall of the chamber, waiting for the Mythrian sentries to pass.

They listened until the sound of the crunching footsteps disappeared completely.

Daniel nodded to Ionica. *Go!* Then turned to Jasper and whispered, "You stay here."

Jasper nodded.

Staying low, they ran for the entrance into the temple dome and ducked inside. A moment later and Jasper followed close behind.

Daniel couldn't believe it. "What did I just say?"

Jasper shrugged.

It was cool and damp inside, the air musty and stale. A shiver ran down Daniel's spine. Assuming it was his uniform trying to adjust to the change in temperature, he set his sleeks to return to their default mode. The hood retracted and the kilt returned.

The creepy feeling, however, did not go away.

What was this place? A labyrinth of passageways obscured the route to the central chamber. More than once, they found themselves diverted to another exit instead of moving deeper into the maze of ruins.

They crept along as fast as they could without making a sound. Except Jasper, who lagged far behind them, humming nervously.

Daniel gave him the evil eye, conveying a single message: *Be quiet!*

A distant voice echoed in from some farther reach of the temple. "Did you hear that?" an Overseer asked in their terrible robotic gibber.

Daniel, Ionica, and Jasper froze.

Waited.

Listened.

Footsteps approached.

Jasper waddled faster than he ever had before as the three of them raced to find somewhere to hide. The entrance to the central chamber loomed large. They raced inside and hugged the walls.

Out in the hall, a pair of Overseers scanned the passageway, glanced into the chamber, but came up empty.

They moved on.

Daniel let himself breathe before taking in where they had ended up. An elaborate structure stood at the heart of the chamber, one of an entirely different scale and design from the rest of the building.

A series of what looked like doorways completely encircled a raised platform. The whole thing appeared to be made out of some dull metal that had grown from a single crystal. There was something distinctly mechanical about it.

"That's the altar," Ionica whispered. "I've seen them before on other planets. They all look the same."

Was this where the thrumming sound had come from?

Several control systems had been set up around the altar, with black bundles of cables and relays snaking their way through one single doorway and up onto the platform, where they diverged through a couple of the other doorways and then abruptly stopped where they had been chopped in half.

"This doesn't make any sense," Ionica said.

Thrummmmmmmmm!

The room shook. Red lights blinked on the consoles.

Jasper made a sound that could only be described as an "uh-oh."

There had to be somewhere to hide. Daniel pointed out a stack of crates and equipment cases. Dashing around behind them, they barely made it in time when the familiar stench of Overseer rot wafted into the room.

"Set it down over there," an Overseer commanded.

Daniel and Ionica peered through the gaps between the

crates. On the altar, three Overseers appeared—literally out of thin air. Two were carrying a large equipment chest between them while the third directed them to where they needed to go.

The two with the chest stepped down off the podium and marched straight for Daniel and Ionica's hiding spot.

The Truth Seekers held their breaths.

The soldiers set the chest down at the foot of the stack, turned on their heels, and abruptly marched out one of the exits.

Daniel exhaled. "That was a close one," he whispered.

Meanwhile, back on the podium, two more Overseers emerged from one of the doorways, again stepping out of nowhere. As before, they lugged heavy equipment, and again they were instructed where to deposit it.

Neither Daniel nor Ionica could believe what they were seeing.

A portal? Ionica mouthed silently.

Could it be? Portals were the stuff of legend. A wormhole through the fabric of space that could be crossed as though stepping through a doorway. No one had ever seen one. There were theories about them; Daniel had learned that much in class. About how they required vast amounts of power to function but nobody knew for sure. Where was the power source for this device?

Another soldier marched in from the outside and stood before the altar.

"Vega Virrus," the soldier announced. "Mimias Lux

reports that he has completed his mission and he requests an audience."

Behind the crates, Ionica grabbed Daniel's wrist and clawed at his skin.

He tried not to cry out in agony.

Virrus was nowhere to be seen, but a response came anyway, in the form of a whisper that everyone in the chamber could hear.

"Did you confirm that the grid is down?"

"It is, sir."

Vega Virrus stepped through the portal and onto the platform, his ragged black cloak drifting in behind him like a nest of vipers. "Begin the landing," he whispered, sweeping past his underling on the way out. "Allow Mimias Lux to make contact."

It took everything Daniel had to hold himself back. Not that he would have survived attacking Virrus and his cohorts, but it would have made him feel better for everything they had put him through.

Reluctantly, Daniel watched them leave.

When the chamber had emptied out again, the two Truth Seekers and the anatom stepped back out into the open.

"Oh, Father," Ionica said. "What have you done?"

Daniel had other priorities. How in all the galaxy did this technology work? "Now we know how they got past Juba's security," he said, approaching the altar with more than a little trepidation. "If they can travel between planets without ships, nowhere is safe."

This close to the machine, Daniel could feel his skin prickle. When he touched the dull metal, it didn't feel as though it were drawing energy from any kind of power source. This was something else. His eyes saw a flat surface, but for a moment it felt as though his fingers were brushing against something far away, across the other side of the galaxy. It was the most impossible sensation.

Excited, Daniel bounded up onto the platform between the doorways.

What he found was truly mind-bending.

Although from the outside, the altar looked like a set of doorframes surrounding a platform, this was all just an optical illusion.

Standing in the middle of the platform, Daniel could suddenly see that a handful of those doorways opened out into other chambers. These chambers couldn't be seen from outside the device, only when standing on the platform at the heart of it. The bundles of cables that appeared to have been cut in half now very obviously carried on through these doorways and into what lay beyond.

"What the Fuse . . ." Daniel felt a little odd up here. A little clammy, but he didn't care. This was too important a discovery.

This was not just *one* portal. This was *many* portals. And it went far beyond the notion of temporary wormholes.

These portals were all part of a device that, to work, had to exist in more than three dimensions. This wasn't just a question of bending space. This was a physical nexus where remote chambers from across the galaxy were permanently joined together and could be accessed like using a revolving door.

"This is a hypercube!" Daniel announced. "And the Sinja found the key to opening it—"

A massive jolt sizzled through Daniel's socket, lighting up every nerve ending. In excruciating agony, he dropped to his knees and cried out.

"Daniel!" Ionica ran to him. "If you're going to be in pain, please be a little quieter about it."

And then she saw it too, the portals that had opened up to reveal other connected destinations. Her mouth hung open.

Jasper paced back and forth in a panic, monitoring the exits for any sudden unwanted visitors.

"I can hear them," Daniel said through gritted teeth.

"Hear who? What are you talking about? If you don't shut up, they'll hear *you*!"

Daniel clawed at his scalp. "They're in my head," he gasped. "The Sinja," he managed to say, his whole body quaking.

A thousand whispers surged and faded, overlapped and crashed, like an ever-present hum, with a single hypnotic message repeated over and over and over—

Obey.

Somehow, the altar had triggered Daniel's socket, enabling it to receive the Sinja commands despite the scrambler in his head. Had the scrambler stopped working? They weren't talking to him; this message was operating on a greater level than just him. They were talking not only to the Overseers here, but every other poor soul under their direction across the entire galaxy.

Daniel fought. With his every breath, he tried rejecting the commands. And with every breath he grew weaker and weaker.

"What do I do?" Ionica begged, completely at a loss as to how she could help him. It all happened when he stepped onto—

"This altar!" she said. "The hypercube. We have to get him away from it. Jasper, help me!" She grabbed Daniel by the shoulders and dragged him across the platform. "Hurry!"

The little anatom did as instructed, plowing his head into Daniel's body and heaving with all his might.

"Scrambler," Daniel managed to say, trying to rub his temple, forcing his skin to peel back to reveal the socket embedded beneath. "Maybe it came loose in the crash."

Ionica peered into the socket. The tiny square chip Astrid had implanted wobbled in its housing.

She scrunched up her eyes. "This is so weird," she said, poking her finger into the opening and pressing the chip back in with a *click.* . . .

The relief was immediate. He could breathe. He could

think. The voices were gone and the shakes had gone with them.

Daniel struggled to sit up. "Jasper," he ordered. "Figure out how to shut these doors in the hypercube. We don't want any more Overseers showing up."

Jasper threw up his wings. How the heck was he supposed to figure that out in five minutes?

Ionica helped Daniel to his feet. "Let's go get my sister," she said.

Daniel couldn't have agreed more.

They made their way over to a far exit, which led back outside, and to the very spot where Vega Virrus and his Overseers were gathering.

Sneaking through the shadows, they could just make out the voices outside when a pair of Overseers rounded the corner, marching toward them.

Caught completely by surprise, for a moment, no one knew what to do.

Then an Overseer reached for his blast-pike.

Sssssnnnnappp!

Electricity arced across the chamber, only to hit a whirling vortex suddenly projected by Daniel's Aegis.

The second Overseer turned and ran.

"Stop him!" Daniel urged. They couldn't afford to let him alert the others!

Whompff!

Ionica projected her vortex shield farther down the

corridor, blocking the Overseer's escape. Then snapped it back, smashing the two Overseers into one another, knocking them completely out.

The two friends didn't dwell. Quietly, they stepped over the bodies and continued on their way.

Approaching the edge of the temple exit, they watched as out on the scorched hardpan of the desert, where Nova still knelt on the ground, a holocule image of Mimias Lux took form before Vega Virrus.

"I've done as you asked," Mimias said. "Juba is yours. Now please. Release my daughter," he begged.

Virrus thought on this for a moment, before rendering his verdict.

"No," he said.

Mimias shook with anger. "That is not what we agreed!"

"There was no agreement. There were orders, and you followed them. Now there are more. You have another daughter. A Truth Secker," Virrus whispered. "Ionica. We've been watching her."

Daniel and Ionica stopped in their tracks and eyed each other.

29

THE BATTLE FOR JUBA

Ionica Lux turned ice-cold.

Without saying a word to Daniel, she calmly strode out of the temple, ignited her Aegis, and taking every tear she had ever shed, every ounce of anger, every measure of hurt—

Whompff!

She blasted Vega Virrus in the back, batting him into the air like a toy. The dark Sinja tumbled end over end and disappeared through a cloud of toxic vapors.

It all happened so fast even Daniel didn't have time to react. It was one of the craziest things he had ever seen, and for once he wasn't the one who had done it.

Nova remained motionless, kneeling amid the chaos.

Realizing that the Overseers were still trying to process

what had just happened, Daniel barreled outside, rotating his toes and spinning around in a complete 360. With one arm outstretched, he slung a wave of incredible power at them from his Aegis before they had a chance to react.

The Overseers toppled like ancient dominoes.

GGRRRRMMMMMMMMM!

Wave after wave of Sinja starfighters howled overhead, diving in steep from orbit and circling back around.

From the north, Truth Seeker Spitfires, Juban Defense Hammers, and War Guild Mustangs zoomed in from the twilight side of Juba to meet them, opening fire in a spectacular blast of light and fury.

Pew, pew, pew, pew, pew! Pew, pew, pew, pew, pew!

Instantly, the sky transformed into a zigzagging maze of energy bolts, with fighters rolling this way and that to avoid getting hit.

WHHHHHOMMMMMMMMM!

A massive fireball streaked across the sky, plowing through the battle, smashing dueling starfighters to pieces, and impacting with the ground just a mile or so away with a thunderous—

KA-BOOOOOOOOOOMMMMMMMMM!

A wall of choking, blinding soil, thrown up into the air like a curtain, suddenly rampaged out in every direction, caught in the shock wave of the blast.

"Look out!" Daniel cried, jumping in front of Nova and throwing up an energy shield to protect her.

The larger debris bounced harmlessly off, but the air, thick with dust, soon had him coughing.

Ionica knelt in front of her sister, studying her as though she were seeing a ghost.

Nova did not react. Her eyes were emotionless; her pale face lacked all expression. She stared into an abyss that only she could see.

"Nova," Ionica said gently, trying to hold it together. "It's me. Io."

Nova said nothing.

"Nova?" Ionica grabbed her big sister by the shoulders, wanting to shake her, to hug her, whatever it took to get her to recognize her. "Come on, Nono," she said, tears dripping down her cheeks. "Get up, please . . . Please."

"She can't answer you!" Daniel cried, looking back over his shoulder. "She's locked in her own head! We have to get her back to the Fortress of Truth!"

Blam! Blam! Blam!

Weapons fire blasted the energy shield, forcing Daniel back a step every time a shot landed.

The swirling dust began to clear. He could see Overseer silhouettes marching toward them.

Daniel readied another massive energy blast.

Pew! Pew! Pew! Pew! Pew!

A Truth Seeker Spitfire, flying low out of the sun, peppered the ground with energy bolts, blasting the Overseers into next week.

"Yes!" Daniel roared. But the relief was short-lived.

Ruuuuuuummmmmmmmmble.

The ground shook and the sky darkened.

Something mechanical was rising up out of the crater, something angular and evil-looking. Something so massive that it made everyone on the ground feel like ants.

SHHHHWOOO-CHKOMMMMMM!

One by one, eight monstrous legs hauled its armored body aloft until it looked for all the galaxy like a fortress being carried on the back of a gargantuan spider. With one gigantic shudder, it began plodding toward the temple.

Daniel's legs turned to rubber. "Ah, we've got a problem," he said.

"I can't get her to move!" Ionica protested.

"Not that!" Daniel cried, pointing at the newest threat. "There's a crawler coming!"

SHHHHWOOO-CHKOMMMMMM!

With every thundering step, the ground quaked and the noise grew as the Battle Armored Sentry Enclosure, known throughout the galaxy as a BASE crawler, made its advance. Designed to secure a tactical position and support an invading army, BASE crawlers stood several stories high. Superficially, this one resembled a gigantic armored spider, but each of them was designed to transport its fortress body effortlessly over the rough terrain.

"Help me!" Ionica begged.

Daniel raced over and together they got Nova to her feet. Her face remained expressionless. She had no comprehension of what was happening.

They gave her a nudge, and Nova started walking. Ionica held her hand and tugged her forward to keep her going in the right direction.

SHHHHWOOO-CHKOMMMMMM!

Daniel pulled up his holographic comms panel. "To any ship within range, we need—"

Daniel hit the dirt hard.

Something had wrapped itself around his ankle. Long, black, ragged fabric. Daniel kicked and squirmed but he couldn't shake it loose. He tried getting to his knees, but another dark tendril shot out of the dust storm and snaked its way around his other foot.

It snapped taut, yanking him facedown into the dirt.

Daniel rolled onto his back.

Vega Virrus had come for him.

"Get her out of here!" Daniel screamed to Ionica. He tore at the rags.

Ionica turned back. Torn between fighting and getting her sister to safety.

Daniel made up her mind for her. "Go!" he yelled.

He dug his clawed fingers into the dirt and tried to hang on, but it was no use. Vega Virrus was too strong.

Without lifting a finger, Virrus stood and watched as the tendrils of his ragged cloak dragged Daniel Coldstar toward him.

30

TRAPPED!

"You don't scare me!" Daniel yelled as the ragged cloak dragged him closer to Vega Virrus.

"A Truth Seeker who lies," Virrus whispered. "A notable improvement."

Whompff!

Daniel sliced through the ragged cloak with a whirling vortex of dirt and debris. He shot up. Vaulting over Virrus. Landing right behind him.

He balled his fist. Wrapped it in Aegis energy. And punched at the deadly Sinja.

Virrus sidestepped without much effort, leaving Daniel wildly off balance.

The advancing BASE crawler lifted another leg.

SHHHHWOOO-CHKOMMMMMM!

The ground shook. Daniel fell in the dirt.

"Why such anger?" Virrus mocked. "What did I do to you to deserve such hatred?"

Was that some kind of joke?

Virrus towered over him. Daniel scrambled backward.

"Who are you, young Truth Seeker?"

"You know who I am!" Daniel spat.

Whompff!

Daniel hurled a spinning disk of energy directly at Virrus. He deflected it away. "I'm Daniel Coldstar."

Virrus considered the name. "Interesting."

Daniel leapt to his feet, his whirling shield held in front. "I doubt you're even real," he goaded. "You're probably another holocule projection like last time."

The last time. Back in the mines. During Daniel's escape, when he first encountered Vega Virrus. The battle had been brutal, but short, and ended as soon as Daniel had used the full power of his Aegis.

Daniel had dreamt of this moment, of facing Virrus again and making him pay for what he had done. Taking him. Putting him in those mines—*everything.*

Virrus stepped forward, held out his hand, and slowly sank it through Daniel's shield.

Daniel panicked. His eyes grew to the size of moons. He'd never seen anything like this.

"I am no apparition," Vega Virrus assured him.

The black tendrils of his cloak snaked their way down

his arm, projected from his fingers, and wrapped themselves around Daniel's throat. They lifted him off his feet. And squeezed.

Daniel kicked and struggled.

SHHHHWOOO-CHKOMMMMMM!

SHHHHWOOO-CHKOMMMMMM!

SHHHHWOOO-CHKOMMMMMM!

The BASE crawler was almost upon them now. Its shadow blotted out the sun.

"Are you the boy who brought me the book?" Virrus whispered.

Why was he doing this? Why was he pretending not to know him?

Daniel jammed his fingers down in between his own throat and Virrus's tightening grip. "You said I would be the greatest Sinja ever," Daniel spat, choking. "You were wrong."

Two more long black tendrils of fabric slithered up Vega Virrus's arm and wrapped themselves around Daniel's wrists. Virrus lowered his arm. The tendrils did all the work now, hoisting Daniel up into the air.

SHHHHWOOO-CHKOMMMMMM!

Daniel gasped, finally able to breathe, while Virrus regarded him as though he were watching a bug he had just caught in a web.

SHHHHWOOO-CHKOMMMMMM!

"Why do you return now?" Virrus asked, puzzled. "You

served your purpose. I have no further use for you."

SHHHHWOOO-CHKOMMMMMM!

"I will stop you, Virrus!" Daniel snarled, struggling against his bonds. "I will free Nova, and Blink. I'll free everyone!"

SHHHHWOOO-CHKOMMMMMM!

"Your anger is misplaced," Virrus remarked evenly. "This is not personal. If it were personal, it would mean that you matter."

The ragged strips of Virrus's cloak swung like an arm, hurling Daniel across the wasteland.

Daniel landed on his feet this time. But Virrus's words had hit harder than any blow could have.

CHKCHKCHKCHKCHK!

He looked up. The BASE crawler had ground to a halt right above him and above the temple.

KA-CLANK! KA-CLANK! KA-CLANK! SHWEEEEEEE!

At the base of each of the crawler's eight enormous legs, the armored plating loosened to allow hidden drills to bore deep into the dirt, securing each leg to the bedrock.

KA-BOOM!

The body of the crawler hurtled to the ground, landing in a cloud of blinding dust, creating an impenetrable fortress that now had sole control over the hypercube lodged inside the ancient temple. Moments later, like castle turrets, the towering crawler legs jettisoned the upper casings around their now-exposed joints to reveal—

194

BLAM! BLAM! BLAM!

Massive defensive cannons unfolded from storage and began blasting ships from the sky.

There was nowhere for Daniel to go. The walls of the crawler were on all sides. He was trapped.

He looked for Virrus, but the Sinja leader was already walking away.

"I know about the *Coldstar*!" Daniel yelled. "I know you're using the grubs as pawns in your sick game!"

Vega Virrus ignored him.

Daniel glanced frantically over at where Virrus was going—the temple. He couldn't see Ionica or her sister, but that didn't mean they had made it to safety.

"Don't ignore me!" Daniel roared.

Virrus kept walking.

Whompff!

Daniel catapulted over Virrus, landing near the entrance to the temple.

"You don't get to forget who I am!" he said.

In one furious motion, Daniel created two spinning vortex shields, one on each arm, and lunged at Virrus.

Sparks flew! Virrus met him with equal force, defending blow after blow from Daniel's frenzied attack.

Daniel swung low, chopping at Virrus's ankles. Then punched high with his other arm, smashing the vortex into Virrus's jaw.

The Sinja was in no mood to play.

Balling his fist, he unleashed. He punched the air, and a massive wave of energy smacked Daniel right through the entrance into the temple.

"I would suggest that you go home," Virrus advised.

"And where is that exactly?" Daniel asked, wiping blood from his nose.

Whompff!

Before Virrus could even answer, Daniel blasted the cracked stone above, bringing the entranceway to the temple crashing down.

Virrus would have to find another way inside.

Daniel scrambled to his feet and hoofed it down the passageway. He'd only bought himself a few extra minutes. He had to make them count.

"Ionica!" he yelled. "Where are you?"

31

THROUGH THE HYPERCUBE

"I'm in here!" Ionica cried.

Daniel raced through the ruined temple, following the echo of her voice.

When he reached the central chamber where Jasper still sat tinkering with the hypercube, he skidded to a halt.

Nova stood completely still, looking as though she had turned to stone. Her tense limbs would not move, even when Ionica tried to hold her hand.

"Oh, no, no, no, no, no," Daniel blurted. "We've got to go. Virrus is, uh, really mad."

Ionica grew desperate. "I don't know what happened. She just came in here and wouldn't take another step."

Daniel edged closer. Something wasn't right. Nova's eyes darted rapidly from side to side. He'd seen that look before when the Overseers filled a grub's head with instructions—

"Get away from her," Daniel warned.

Nova's head twitched and her eyes settled on her little sister. "Io," she said softly.

Ionica couldn't contain her joy. "Yes!" she cried. "Yes! It's me!"

Nova smiled, a warm, comforting smile, so familiar and full of love that Ionica never saw the blow coming.

Ionica's head rocked back and she collapsed, unconscious.

"Well, this is just great," growled Daniel, torn between helping Ionica and stopping Nova from doing whatever she was about to do.

Nova made the decision for him. She grabbed her helmet, which still dangled by its umbilical plugged into her socket, pulled it down over her head, and turned to face him.

"Nova," Daniel urged, holding up his hands. "Remember me? Remember the pit? You helped me. You always helped me. Now I'm here to help you. I know you hear those voices in your head. You do not have to obey them. Fight them!"

Because if she didn't fight them, he'd be fighting her.

But Nova did not fight it. Grabbing her sister by the utility belt, she lifted Ionica and carried her like a sack of Yanill potatoes into the hypercube.

"Stop!" Daniel cried, leaping to block her way.

Nova didn't even hesitate. Dropping Ionica, she swung at Daniel with all the power that her ancient Mythrian power armor held.

Whompff!

Daniel took the blow to his Aegis shield. He skidded backward. Righted himself. Then slammed right into her.

It was like hitting a wall. His legs buckled.

Nova swung again, but Daniel was quicker this time. He ducked. Came up. Ducked again. The two of them circled each other, trading blows.

There had to be a way to get her to snap out of this. There had to be.

Jasper skirted around the edge of the platform, trying to stay out of trouble. When Nova went one way, he went the other. It was a good plan until he ran straight into her legs.

Again, not even a flicker of hesitation slowed Nova's reactions. She kicked the little anatom out of the way.

Now was Daniel's chance!

He charged at her, only to find Ionica struggling to get up and block his way.

"Don't hurt her," she said, but Daniel couldn't stop himself now even if he wanted to.

He plowed on and the three of them careened right through one of the open portals—tumbling headfirst into another world.

Immediately, Daniel's senses lit up. His ears throbbed

from the sudden change in air pressure. The stink of this new planet made him want to gag. How far he had just traveled across the galaxy in the blink of an eye was anyone's guess.

He stumbled, and then got up, only to have Nova strike him again and again.

He snatched at her armor. Hooked his foot around the back of her ankle, and together they tumbled down a sharp incline, colliding with mossy rocks and rebounding over fallen walls, trading blows in a bizarre slow-motion tussle.

Daniel felt sick. His stomach gurgled as though his breakfast were trying to come up and pay him a visit. This was insane. It was the gravity, he realized. It was so much lighter on this planet than anything he was used to.

Nova jabbed her armored elbow into his face. It crunched. His head snapped back. His feet lifted up. He tumbled backward, arms flailing.

When he landed, he planted his feet. Tried to get control. Went to run at Nova, but vaulted into the air instead and just kept going.

Whoosh!

The massive tail spikes of a Hammertail whipped beneath his feet.

Where the heck did that come from?

Daniel craned his neck, mid-flight. A saddled-up Hammertail in war paint snapped around. It had targeted Daniel, but battered Nova instead, knocking her out cold.

She sailed away, landing in a heap.

Where was Ionica? She had to be somewhere.

There! She was out cold again, a little ways down the slope from the hypercube—

Daniel landed with a bounce, expecting another swipe from the Hammertail, but it didn't come. The animal seemed to have about as much experience in this kind of low-gravity environment as he did. Unable to stop its own momentum, the animal spun around until it was so dizzy, it collapsed onto its knees.

And that was when Daniel realized the scope of his predicament. There were Overseers *everywhere*, wrestling unsuccessfully with herds of trabasaurs across a rocky moorland dotted with lichens and pungent heather.

The hypercube at the center of this planet's temple com plex sat up on the hill behind him. While the entire area was enclosed behind the massive walls of another BASE crawler, just like on Juba.

Daniel had to get out of the open before his luck ran out. The Overseers were in such a chaotic mess trying to corral their mounts that they hadn't even noticed him. Yet.

Blast it! More Overseers were heading up there now. He'd never get to Ionica in time. He opened a channel. "Ionica, wake up," he growled.

"Just five more minutes," she moaned.

"Wake up now or you're dead."

He watched her head suddenly pop up as she took in her

surroundings. He signaled to her to stay low and get out of there.

Grrrrrrr!

The angry Hammertail had gotten back up onto its feet. Not as big as Alice, but just as intimidating. Daniel couldn't tell if it was a male or a female, and he wasn't about to ask if he could take a look.

The beast's nostrils flared. It pawed the ground. It had Daniel in its sights, and it had no intention of missing this time.

"Wait a minute. . . ." Daniel rummaged around in the pouches of his utility belt until his fingers wrapped themselves around a sticky bar of Tawanga. Alice would be so mad if he knew Daniel was sharing his favorite snack with some strange Hammertail, but this was an emergency.

He wafted the chewy stick of dried fruit and bugs at it. "Here," he said. "It's all yours if you want it."

He tossed it over to the suspicious beast.

The Hammertail sniffed it. Licked it.

And liked it. *Really* liked it.

It glanced up.

"Yes," Daniel said, already holding out another piece, his hand shaking. "There's more."

The ripe-smelling trabasaur ambled over, looking Daniel right in the eye as if to say, *Okay, I won't kill you today.*

"So what's your name?" Daniel asked, keeping his voice soothing and calm. It was a lie.

The Hammertail edged closer and ate out of his hand. Good, they were making a connection. Daniel ran his fingers gently over its muzzle and firmly took hold of the bridle. The Hammertail didn't react.

"I think we're going to be good friends," he said, pretending to relax. "Don't you?"

He glanced around to see how Ionica was doing. She kept low, zigzagging her way from rock to rock until she made it down without being spotted.

He did his best to keep the Hammertail calm while she crept up to join him.

"I think we're on borrowed time here, don't you?" she said, rubbing her head. "Boy, that hurt."

"One thing's for sure, we can't go back through that hypercube. We'll have to find another way off this rock."

"What planet is this, anyway?" she wondered.

"You know, I forgot to ask. Come on."

Tugging on the bridle, he led the trabasaur in Nova's direction, using its enormous body to shield them from the view of the Overseers. The animal seemed content to follow his commands for now. Daniel would have to wait and see how long that lasted.

Approaching Nova's prone body sprawled out on the ground, Ionica said, "What did you do to my sister?"

"You're welcome. She was trying to kill you. Remember?" Daniel stumbled and clung to the saddle as he walked beside the beast.

"Walk slower," Ionica suggested. "You're not used to the gravity. Your legs are too strong here, you'll keep flying up."

"It's—awkward," he said with a grunt. He found that skipping seemed to work best.

When they reached Nova, he tapped her with the toe of his boot. She really was out.

Ionica smacked him out of the way and knelt down at her side. "Oh, Nono, what did they do to you?"

Daniel watched the Overseers and trabasaurs, all still fixated on whatever it was the Sinja had ordered. Their luck wasn't going to last forever. "Can we talk about this later? We need to get out of here."

"Help me get her up," Ionica said.

"And do what?"

She thumbed at the Hammertail. "Tie her on like a saddlebag. You got a better idea?"

When they were finished, Nova dangled awkwardly, but as long as she didn't wake up, this would work.

"There's our exit," said Daniel, keeping his voice down.

An enormous gate in the BASE crawler wall stood wide open. The craggy landscape beyond looked empty but promising.

Daniel led Ionica and the Hammertail slowly out of the Sinja encampment when all he wanted to do was run. Any moment now, he expected to get caught, yet somehow he kept right on walking. Reminding himself that he could panic later, if he had time. Eventually, unbelievably, they crossed out into the plain and walked right out the door.

Daniel wanted to laugh. He let out a long, slow breath.

Ionica shook her head. "I can't believe we just walked out of there. The Sinja are so arrogant," she said, "they never even considered that someone could infiltrate their precious base."

Daniel glanced back over his shoulder.

A sly grin tugged at his lips.

A couple of miles out beyond the walls, the open sky was streaked with orange. Pillars of rock towered on the horizon. Plants that appeared too weak to support their own bulk stood in freakishly tall clumps, dotted around the moorland.

Ionica swiped at her holographic display and tried to open a channel again.

> BLOCKED <

"What the heck?"

"Still no signal?" Daniel asked.

"We have local comms, but all long-range communications on or off this planet are being blocked," she said.

She brought up a galactic map in the hope that it could tell her where they were, but that didn't work either. It couldn't connect to a hub, and just flashed one message repeatedly:

> YOUR LOCATION IS UNKNOWN <

Angrily, she swiped the display away. "Doesn't make any sense."

Daniel rubbed the back of the Hammertail's head.

"What do you think? What do we do now, huh?"

The Hammertail grunted. Not the way Alice would have, but just enough that it felt like a response. A really crabby one.

"Do you have a name?" Daniel wondered. "I have to call you something."

The Hammertail snorted, irritated.

"Chuckles it is," Daniel agreed.

Ionica simply stared at him. "Seriously. You're going to talk to the Hammertail now?"

Daniel shrugged. "Hey, he got us out of there. Besides, we're short of friends around here." He surveyed the sky. "Maybe if we wait until nightfall the stars might be able to tell us where we are."

"Assuming this planet even has a nightfall," she said.

"Look on the bright side," Daniel said. "We're safe. For now. We'll figure out a way to get home."

Home. Huh.

He'd never thought of the Fortress of Truth as home before now.

Ahead, a series of rolling hills sat some distance away. Rocky outcroppings hugged their crests like stone spines.

"Looks promising," Daniel said. "What do you think?"

Ionica went to answer, but it was only belatedly that she realized he was talking to his new pal. She rolled her eyes.

Chuckles didn't say much either. Neither did Nova, for that matter. She was still out. She swung from the saddle hooks, her head lolling into the trabasaur's ribs.

Ionica watched her, but her expression was hard for Daniel to read. Was that joy on her face? Or fear? Or a little bit of both? Seeing her sister like this, seeing her at all, it had to be difficult.

"What am I going to do when she wakes up?" Ionica said.

"She'll attack you first chance she gets," he reminded her. "I'd at least tie her hands together. Give yourself a head start."

"You make that sound like I'll be dealing with this on my own."

"Hey, I learned my lesson. I'm not coming between two sisters ever again."

He climbed up into the saddle and took out his trinoculars. Distance readings scrolled down the side of the viewfinder. The hills were another couple of miles away and littered with boulders.

"Well, let's see what we got," Daniel said, getting comfortable in the saddle. "There's definitely a few places we can hide out at over there—ugh, forget it. . . . Blast it! *More* Overseers."

"How many?"

"Enough."

The Overseers had gathered at the foot of a hill. One of them had a blast-pike aimed at a couple of unusually tall-looking travelers who had been cooking around an open fire. When the tip of his weapon flared, they shot up, hands in the air, while the other Overseers tore down their camp, and kicked dirt into the hearth.

The travelers didn't react, they were too cowed, too intimidated. A small child came running down toward them, crying. Daniel realized why when he shifted his focus. Huts and houses had been erected farther up the hillside, sandwiched in between the rocks and lashed to platelike outcroppings. There was an entire village up there! Filled with frightened faces peering out from the shadows, hoping that this would all just go away.

Blam! Blam!

The Overseers started firing. Daniel flinched, expecting to see carnage, but they weren't firing at the travelers. They were firing directly into the hillside—into the ground. And in response?

Slowly, the ground stood up.

32

ON THE BACKS OF GIANTS

These were not hills at all.

These were Barbatanas. *Barbatana titanis trabasauri* to be exact; the largest known trabasaurs in the galaxy.

"I read about these!" Daniel said, amazed. "I never thought I'd actually get to see one up close!" Barbatanas only lived in low-gravity environments like this one, which over time had allowed these creatures to develop truly epic proportions.

One by one, these massive beasts rose up, heaving their gargantuan bodies into the air. They stretched for over a quarter of a mile from head to tail and stood over thirty stories high. A blanket of moss and lichens grew on their backs in a symbiotic relationship that kept the animals protected, and nourished their guests.

The village dwellings that were lashed to their backs

flexed and shook with the sudden movement, but otherwise held fast. The people living in them generally went about their business as though this were all perfectly normal.

Each slow, thunderous step of the Barbatanas shook the ground beneath them, raining soil down on the Overseers, who scattered in every direction.

Smaller trabasaurs and other assorted creatures emerged from their resting spots to join the nomadic train on its forced journey deeper into the wilderness.

"This is perfect," Daniel said. "All we have to do is tag along and blend in. Just another wanderer."

"Assuming they don't rat us out to the Overseers," Ionica warned. "We don't know if we can trust them."

"Do we have any other choice?" he said. "Get on."

He helped Ionica climb behind him, then seized their opportunity. He snapped the reins and pushed Chuckles into a full gallop. The Hammertail rocketed across the moorland, its feet barely touching the ground.

The last Barbatana in the train was a little slower than the rest, which gave them just enough time to catch up and tuck in under the shadow of its colossal tail.

Ionica grew jumpy. "Be careful of its butt, please."

Daniel was about to ask why when he found out the hard way. A giant cavity opened up and Chuckles-sized poop began tumbling to the ground with a monumental *splat!*

"You know, they track their animals," a distant voice

explained. "You will not lose them for long if you wish to hide."

"Wow. This has to be the shortest attempt at blending in, in history," Ionica mused. "Nice work."

Daniel ignored her. Embarrassed, he glanced up. Way, way, up high, to where a tall, thin boy with shimmering bronze skin stood at the rails of an observation platform secured to the back of the creature. Blaser cannons were mounted at strategic points on the deck. Daniel was glad they hadn't opened fire.

"How did you know we were here?" Daniel called back.

The boy shrugged. "I've been watching you since you left their compound."

Daniel's shoulders sagged.

A small figure waddled up to the railing and waved a flipper.

"Also, your anatom told me."

Daniel raked his fingers through his hair, both frustrated and elated. For an anatom whose top speed was waddle, Jasper was exceedingly fast. How in the world had he gotten ahead? *Again.* "Jasper! How do you *do* that?"

The penguin shrugged.

"Come," the boy urged, throwing down a rope ladder. "It is best if you let that creature go."

"Nice thought, but we can't climb up that carrying Nova, even in such low gravity," Ionica said. She called up. "Can you throw us a line?"

Aghast, the boy regarded the Mythrian soldier dangling from the saddle hooks with a mixture of fear and disgust. "Why bring that?" he said. "It brings danger."

"She's my sister," she said.

"I am very sorry to hear that."

Reluctantly, the boy did as he was asked.

Daniel rubbed the Hammertail behind the ear. "Well, thanks for the ride, Chuckles," he said. "Some advice, friend to friend? Don't go back. Have your own adventure."

Chuckles snorted and trotted off, never once looking back.

33

THE WANDERING VILLAGE

Tau Soto was ten years old and he was already a man.

The elders had said so because he killed a Ganoush with his bare hands. Tau made a point of sharing this fact at least three times in a span of five minutes. "Very dangerous animal," he said. "Very dangerous." He waved his arms in the air and roared.

Daniel leaned in close to Ionica and whispered, "What's a Ganoush?"

She shrugged. "I don't know, but don't belittle him. He's obviously very proud of his achievement," she whispered back. "He's trying to impress you. Just tell him what a good boy he is and move on."

"Think that'll work?"

"Of course! I do it to you all the time."

Daniel did a double take before turning back to Tau. "We're grateful for your help," he said.

"You are welcome," said Tau. "Any enemy of the Sinja is a friend of mine."

Daniel appreciated the sentiment, but one thing he had learned as a Truth Seeker this past year was that the enemy of your enemy was not necessarily your friend.

For a ten-year-old boy, Tau was tall—at least two heads taller than Daniel—with long limbs that looked as though they'd been stretched like rubber.

Together they dragged Nova across the lookout platform anchored to the back of the Barbatana's tail and set about chaining her hands to a post situated behind a fluttering cloth windbreak.

When they were finished, Tau stood with his hands on his hips, glancing from Nova to Ionica and back again. "You always do this to your sister?"

"It's complicated," she replied.

"This is a very strange family," Tau noted.

Jasper nodded in agreement.

Ionica knelt down and gently removed Nova's helmet. She set the fearsome mask down, careful not to dislodge the umbilical that linked it to Nova's own socket, buried in her temple.

Tau gasped. "I have never seen one unmasked before. She is so young. I thought they were warriors!"

Daniel shook his head. "They're just kids. Like us. They all are."

Nova looked so peaceful, as though everything that had happened to her had melted away. Ionica couldn't help herself. She reached out and stroked her sister's cheek. "I can't believe she's alive," she said. She glanced up at Daniel. "How do we do this?"

"Are you sure you want to try? You saw what happened to me," Daniel reminded Ionica. He could still feel the searing pain in his head, just thinking about it.

Tears welled in Ionica's eyes. "I don't know any other way of getting her back."

He gestured for her to move over and knelt down by Nova's umbilical. He looked it over. It wasn't permanently attached. All he had to do was give it a twist. He just had no idea what it would do to anyone who had been connected to one of these things for a year.

Tau kept his distance. "Do you know what you are doing?"

"No," Daniel said. He glanced up at their new companion, hopeful. "Do you?"

Tau backed away. "Why would I know what to do?"

Worth a shot. Oh well. "This is how the Sinja control them," Daniel explained. He sighed. "Well, here goes nothing."

He gave the umbilical a sharp twist at the socket and eased it out of Nova's head.

For one brief, shining moment, Nova remained peacefully unconscious.

Then the convulsions began.

The shaking was violent and relentless. Her legs, her

arms, her entire body twisted and contorted. Foam seeped from her twitching mouth.

"Put it back!" Ionica cried.

"No, wait!" Daniel protested, but Ionica was faster.

Grabbing the umbilical, Ionica plugged it straight back into Nova's socket. It didn't make any difference. Her seizures only worsened.

"What have you done?" Daniel panicked. "You're going to kill her!"

"I just wanted it to stop!"

Daniel grabbed Nova by the shoulders and tried to pin her down. "Nova," he said. "Wake up! Nova!"

Nova's eyes snapped open. Still convulsing sharply, she looked at Daniel with cold, dead eyes. And then she stopped moving.

She sat there, chained to the post, as though nothing had happened.

Ionica shoved him out of the way. "Nono, look at me." She tried to smile. "Nono?"

Slowly, deliberately, Nova turned her attention to her little sister.

Then she lunged at her, like a wounded animal.

Ionica jumped back. Nova's chains snapped taut.

Daniel rubbed his hand over his mouth. "There has to be a way to do this," he said. "You okay?"

Ionica licked her wounds. "I'm just glad the chains didn't snap."

"Very strong chains," Tau announced proudly. "I used them to kill a Ganoush."

A voice, deep and booming, called out from the back of the Barbatana.

Daniel glanced through a gap in the canvas windbreak. At the end of the long rope walkway leading up to the village secured to the Barbatana's rocky plates, an impossibly tall adult ducked as he stepped out from one of the gently rolling dwellings.

He called again.

"Who's that?" asked Daniel. "Do you think he can help us?"

Tau's face drained of all color. "Oh no," he said.

The man raised his hand to signal the boy.

"Stay down," Tau urged.

"What's going on?" asked Daniel, for once doing as he was told.

"He is the Wanax of our chorio," Tau said, which explained nothing. He held up his hand and called back.

The Wanax seemed annoyed, and before long he and Tau were having a superheated conversation in a language that Daniel didn't recognize.

"I have to go," Tau explained, despondent. "I have to finish my homework."

"The Wanax is a teacher?" Ionica asked.

"The Wanax is like a leader of a house."

That made even less sense to Daniel. "Why would a

Wanax care if you haven't done your homework?"

Tau rolled his eyes. "He is also my father."

Tau retrieved his pack from a hook and slung it over his narrow shoulders.

"Hey, by the way," Daniel prodded. "What planet are we on?"

Tau seemed incredulous. "How can you not know which planet you are on?"

"We didn't get here the normal way," Ionica explained.

Tau shrugged. "You are on Massif. Outer territory of the Bantu Worlds."

She was shocked. "The Bantu Worlds are powerful. They'd never let the Sinja just take over one of their own!"

"The Sinja have made our worlds believe that Massif is under quarantine and should be avoided to prevent the spread of disease."

"How?"

"They turned our leader against us." Tau went to walk away, but Daniel was still chewing on the information.

"Does he have kids?"

Tau didn't seem to understand why Daniel would ask such a curious question. "*She* used to, yes."

Daniel glanced over at Ionica. She shook her head gently, finally starting to understand the extent of the Sinja conspiracy. "So her kids were taken too, and are in a mine somewhere."

"Probably." Daniel glanced up at Tau. "Hey, if Massif is

under quarantine? Does that mean all spaceports are—?"

"Closed. There are no spaceports," the boy replied with a derisive laugh. "No one gets on or off Massif. Except you two, it seems. Now," he said. "Keep your heads down. Stay out of sight. My people will not appreciate me bringing one of those soldiers on board, even if she is your sister."

34

NIGHT VISION

Daniel, Ionica, and Jasper tinkered with Nova's connection to the Sinja network long after the sun sank beneath the jagged horizon.

The air chilled sharply, pinching at Daniel's fingers. The delicious aroma of roasting meat wafted down from the dwellings, making his mouth water. He would have to make do with a ration bar, and if that wasn't enough, he could always eat Alice's Tawanga. On an empty stomach, Alice's favorite dried-bug snack didn't seem so bad. He was suddenly glad he always had some with him.

Working by the light of the bioluminescent lanterns that hung from post hooks along the length of the Barbatana's back, they kept Nova tied up with more ropes than were probably needed. But at least she couldn't lunge at them again.

Her creepy staring was another matter.

"It's like she's another person," Ionica said, spooked.

"She *is* another person," Daniel said. "The real Nova is in there somewhere; we just have to get to her."

Slicing Nova's umbilical open down its entire length revealed a tangle of components that were difficult to make sense of. Jasper spliced himself into the network, and fed the data to Daniel's holographic control console.

Sinja network commands popped onto the screen like a hailstorm. There was only one problem.

"I can't see any way to disable this thing using code, can you?" Daniel said.

Ionica shook her head as she pointed out a series of commands. "Look, the code's booby-trapped. Who knows what'll happen if we tamper with it."

Jasper sniffed and gently touched his flipper to Daniel's temple.

"I can't," Daniel said, dismissing him.

Jasper tried again.

"What's he trying to say?" she asked.

"My scrambler. Look," he said, explaining it to the anatomic penguin as though talking to a small child. "If I remove it and give it to Nova, I have to put something in its place, or I'm dead, or worse."

"What about swapping chips?" Ionica suggested. "You take her Identifier, she takes your scrambler."

Daniel looked at her like he'd just been stabbed in the back. "What?"

"It wouldn't be forever," Ionica pleaded. "You spent an entire year with your Identifier still in place. It would just need to be long enough to get her disconnected from this Sinja mind control. Maybe then you can swap it back."

"Maybe," Daniel agreed. "Or maybe not. I was never under mind control—they never got that far. I don't know what it'll do to her."

"We can't leave her like this," Ionica insisted. "If she gets loose and she's still under their control—we're dead."

Jasper gesticulated furiously until quite suddenly Daniel's holographic display flickered; there was an incoming message.

At first, the squiggles and lines of the message were nothing more than gibberish, accompanied by discordant musical notation.

Then the display wiped itself clean and two words appeared in simple text. The words were from Jasper.

Only way, the anatom said.

"Wait. You can *write*?"

Jasper shrugged.

"So why didn't you do it before now?" he snapped.

Jasper shrugged again. You never asked.

"If we do this, you know what this means, right?"

Jasper nodded. On Daniel's holographic display the words Save Life appeared.

Daniel glowered. "I mean, this has to be quick. Real quick. You understand?" he said.

Jasper nodded.

Daniel turned to Ionica. "This is temporary."

"I understand," she said.

"Once we think she's no longer under their control, I get my scrambler back. Otherwise, I have no protection from Overseers looking to control *me*."

"Got it."

"And we only have a few seconds before either of us goes into shock. Five seconds, tops. You got *that*?"

"Yes," she said. "I understand. And Daniel?"

He braced himself for another smart-mouthed comment.

"Thank you."

He squirmed. "Well, uh, all right then," Daniel said uneasily. He tapped the side of his head, prompting his skin to peel back, revealing his socket.

He leaned forward, gazing into Nova's eyes, hoping to see some sign of the girl he knew in the mines. Was she still in there?

She snarled at him.

That was all the motivation Daniel needed. He firmly set his jaw and yanked the umbilical out of her head.

One.

Nova blinked, a familiar moment of disorientation settling over her.

Two.

Daniel deftly reached into the socket and snatched her Identifier out before she could react.

Three.

He reached into his own socket and tugged the scrambler

free. A sharp pain bolted through his head. Daniel winced.

Four.

His hands shook. He held the scrambler out. It tumbled from his fingers and slid to the edge of the platform.

Ionica snatched it up before it was lost forever.

Five.

Sharp, violent convulsions racked Nova's entire body as though she had been wired into a power supply. Her bindings strained to contain her. Her head snapped from side to side with such force it was a wonder she didn't break her own neck.

Using both hands, Daniel struggled to keep Nova's head still while Ionica eased the scrambler chip into the correct housing.

She missed once, twice. "Hold her still!" she complained.

Daniel had other problems. Electricity shot into his brain. Stars blistered his eyeballs. Needles jabbed into every nerve ending from his toes all the way up to his hair. "Hurry up," he said. "I need to get my own socket taken care of!" He clamped his eyes shut, but the tears squeezed through anyway.

She tried again. Felt the familiar *click* of the device slotting into place, and completely forgot about Daniel's predicament as she witnessed a moment of peace sweeping over her sister.

Daniel struggled with inserting Nova's Identifier into his socket and took a moment to catch his breath. "Thanks for the help," he quipped, but his annoyance was soon forgotten when he realized that something magical was happening.

Ionica watched her sister as though searching her soul.

Nova watched her right back, her eyes bulging as though she'd been yanked from a deep sleep. And then a sense of wonder overwhelmed her.

"Io?" she said. "Is that you?"

And then the little girl who had lost her big sister, the little girl who missed her so much, who had become a Truth Seeker in her honor; that little girl returned. And she was happy, and she was smiling, and her dark eyes were filled with big, wet tears, and they were tears of joy. And she said, "Yes, Nono, it's me. . . ."

Ionica Lux threw her arms around her big sister and squeezed with all her might.

Nova kissed her hair. "I would hug you back," she whispered, "but I seem to be a little tied up."

"Oh, right!" Daniel said. He reached over and loosened her bindings.

Nova rubbed her wrists, trying to make the red marks go away. "Who are you?"

"Daniel," he said.

"Who?"

"Daniel Coldstar?" Didn't she recognize him? "We were in the relic mines together?"

None of this seemed familiar to her.

"You used to visit me in the pit?" Daniel added, starting

to get his strength back. "You'd bring me food."

"Sorry."

Wow, that hurt. "Boy, you sure got socked in the socket," he said.

"Where am I?" she asked. Ionica helped her to her feet.

"Massif," Ionica explained.

"Massif . . . ?" A clear sense of dread seemed to take hold of her. She panicked. "Massif? No, we can't be here," she said. "We can't."

"It'll be okay," Ionica reassured her.

"No it won't!" she insisted. "You don't understand. The things they made me do. . . ." Her voice trailed away before the memories could consume her.

And that was when it was her turn for the tears to flow, spilling hot down her cheeks in a tsunami of uncontrolled emotions.

She threw her arms around her sister and wept into her neck.

Ionica rocked her and let her cry it out. But when Nova opened her eyes and really saw that the wilderness through which the train of Barbatanas was negotiating was bathed in a hard, silvery light from artificial structures looming on the horizon, when she saw what looked like a city of hard lines and harsher shadows—that was when the horror gripped her.

"We have to leave," she said.

35

HOUSE OF SOTO

Daniel spied the Sinja stronghold through his trinoculars. "I don't believe it," he said. "So this is where they've been hiding out all this time?"

On the horizon, the familiar lines of the enormous Sinja fleet that he had witnessed leaving Musa Degh sat interconnected, amid ground fortifications. These were the ships that had been loaded up with the thousands of mind-controlled grubs who now wore Mythrian armor.

They all had to be there. Right now. Everyone he'd ever known.

Maybe even Blink.

Daniel handed the trinoculars to Ionica. "I have an idea," he said.

"I'm afraid to hear it," she said, taking a look for herself.

"They have ships," he explained.

"Obviously."

"No, not those ones. They have fighters, transports. Smaller ships of all kinds." It was so obvious! "Why not just walk in and take one? We'll be jumping to Inspinity before they know it."

Ionica slapped the trinoculars back in his hand. "You expect us to walk into a Sinja fortress and just steal one of their ships?"

"Not us. Me. They don't know we're here."

"It'll never work." She turned to Jasper. "Come on, let's put Daniel's scrambler back—"

Daniel gripped her wrist. "Wait."

Ionica eyed him uncertainly.

"Nova's Identifier," he said. "What if I keep it? If they think I'm her, what will stop me? They'll let me straight through the front door. I'm pretty sure I can fit in her armor—"

"Are you crazy?" Ionica roared in disbelief. "You think you can fool the entire Sinja military?"

Daniel shrugged. "No. Just the guards at the front door."

"Then what?"

Far ahead, what sounded like someone banging on a hollow log echoed through the night. Moments later, the lookout on the next Barbatana in the train answered back with a similar beat, until one by one the message made its way down the chain.

"What's that?" Nova asked.

From one of the dwellings anchored farther up on the Barbatana's back, Tau emerged. "A patrol is coming!" he called, making his way down to them.

"We need to turn around!" Nova urged.

Tau threw up his hands. "What you are asking is not possible. Do you see anyone steering this beast? One does not tell a Barbatana where to go. One encourages him to move. After that, one follows."

"But we're heading right for that Sinja base," she said.

Tau shrugged. "Yes, this happens from time to time."

"What's it like in there?" Daniel pressed. "Is there much security?"

Tau threw back his head and laughed. "There are thousands of soldiers," he said. "It is a very dangerous place."

"What about ships?"

"Hundreds. Whole squadrons."

Ionica rolled her eyes.

Tau was quick on the uptake. "If you are planning on stealing a ship, it is a very worthy plan. They have the only ships that are permitted to fly on Massif."

"See?" Daniel gave her a smug grin.

"Getting there alive will be a much bigger problem," Tau explained excitedly.

Daniel went back to studying the layout through his trinoculars. "I can do this," he insisted. And then Daniel saw it. Nestled at the center of the compound was the peculiar dome-like structure called the chronoscope that he had seen in the relic mines.

"Wait a minute. . . ." Was that the machine Vega Virrus had used to–?

Daniel whirled on Nova. "The Book of Planets is *here*?"

Nova shifted uneasily. "Yes, it's here," she replied.

Tau tried his best to understand. "What is so special about this book?"

Daniel reluctantly explained, his face ashen. "It helped the Sinja get past Massif's defenses. It's brought war to every corner of the galaxy." He looked down at his feet. "And it's my fault that they have it."

Tau looked like he'd been stabbed through the heart.

"I have to make this right," Daniel begged.

"People are dead," said Tau, unrestrained disgust filling his voice. "Members of my family are dead."

"A lot more people will die if I don't fix this," Daniel said. He turned on Ionica. "All I have to do is walk in there and take it."

"First a ship, now *that*? You're crazy!" Ionica cried. "Daniel, you'll die! Even if you could make it *in* there you'll never make it *out* alive!"

"How often does an opportunity like this just wander by?"

Tau inclined his head. "Technically, we are the ones just wandering by, but–"

"You know what I mean," he snapped. "If we can take

away their power, we end this chaos in a heartbeat," Daniel persisted.

Nova forcefully inserted herself into the conversation. "You think chaos is what they're after? Chaos is their distraction."

Ionica eyed her sister. "What are you talking about? A distraction from what?"

"Their search for the Twelve," Daniel said. "Your father told me that they were looking for the Twelve."

"What is this Twelve?" asked Tau.

Daniel shrugged. "I don't know," he said. "But I bet she does."

Nova swallowed hard.

"The Twelve are planets scattered throughout the galaxy that are connected to each other. Massif, Juba, Fclonis."

"Connected how? Through the hypercube?"

"It's more than that, but I don't know the details."

The hairs on the back of Daniel's neck stood on end. "Why are the Twelve so important?"

"I don't know," Nova replied, turning away.

"What are they going to do with them once they find them all?"

"I don't know!"

That wasn't good enough. "*Have* they found them all?" Daniel pressed.

"No," Nova admitted. "I don't think so."

Daniel chewed on what she had to say. "If they haven't

found all twelve of these planets, then, whatever their plans, getting the Book of Planets back would stop them dead in their tracks. I *have* to do this," Daniel said.

"And what are we supposed to do while you're gone?" Ionica protested. "Just sit around?"

"No. You need to figure out how to get past this long-range communications blockade and send a distress call to the Truth Guild, the War Guild, the Bantu Warriors, and anyone else who will listen."

Ionica's jaw dropped. "How the heck am I supposed to do that? I don't have a ship to get high enough above the comms-dampening field!"

"You're a skyrider," Daniel said. "Skyride."

"No one's ever gone that high, not even Hella Phad!"

"Maybe she never tried. Maybe she never had to. But she taught you everything she knows, didn't she?"

Nova and Tau had absolutely no idea what this all meant. "Uh, what's a skyrider?" Nova asked.

"Ask your sister. Now, take your armor off."

Ionica shook her head. "Hold your trabasaurs. Tau, you got anything she can wear?" Daniel didn't seem to under-stand. "Well, I'm not letting her sit here naked."

A little while later, Tau returned with a bundle of clothes in his arms—undershirts, kaftans, leggings, and two pairs of boots. "I did not know her size," he explained.

"Thank you," said Nova.

The Mythrian armor took some effort to pry off Nova's

body, as though it were a parasite refusing to give up its host. Inside the metal cladding, pressure sleeves adjusted to the size of the wearer's limbs so that virtually anyone could wear the armor, from a child to an adult; they would all look the same from the outside.

There was just one tiny problem.

The chest plate would not seal with Daniel's Aegis still attached.

"I told you, you need to take that thing off," Ionica said.

"I can't," Daniel objected.

Tau did not understand. "This is a strange time to be so attached to an inanimate object."

"No, I mean I physically can't do it. It won't let me."

"Of course it will," Ionica persisted. "You have to let it."

Ever since Daniel had discovered the Truth Seeker weapon in the relic mines, it had secured itself to his chest and refused to leave his body. It guarded his life. It protected him day and night. In over a year he had never been without his Aegis. It was with him in the shower. It was with him while he slept. It had saved his life countless times. It was a part of him now. Truth be told, he wasn't sure he wanted to be without it.

A yawning sense of emptiness rose up from his gut. He glanced down at the ancient silver relic and held it gently.

Daniel closed his eyes. Torin had taught him that he had to think with his head and his heart to control his Aegis. Certainly, he'd mastered the technique to the point that he could defend himself with ease.

But every time he tried to remove the weapon, something inside him screamed.

It couldn't happen now. Not now.

He wanted to stop the war. Stop the Sinja. He wanted to make up for the chaos he had unwittingly helped unleash. That's what his heart wanted.

And his mind knew that in order to do that, he had to step into the heart of that Sinja fortress and retrieve the Book of Planets.

Daniel tensed his fingers around the rim of his silver Aegis and pulled it away from his chest.

He opened his eyes. He'd done it. The Aegis sat in the palm of his hand, and the pressure on his chest was gone.

Despite wearing a suit of ancient alien armor, he felt naked.

"See?" Ionica said.

Daniel handed the weapon to Nova. "Look after this," he said. "Maybe Ionica can show you a couple of moves. But I'll be back for it."

He sealed the armored chest plate and stood up. With every movement, every twitch of his muscles, the suit responded, augmenting his strength to superhuman levels. No wonder Nova had kicked his butt so easily.

Ionica handed him the helmet.

Daniel wasted no time in ripping the umbilical out completely. "So we're all clear on the plan, right?"

Ionica nodded. "You're going to walk to your death

trying to steal back a relic and an escape ship. I'm going to get blasted out of the sky trying to get a message out past the long-range-comms blockade—"

"And *we're* going to create a distraction, on the off chance either of you makes it," Nova said, patting Tau on the back.

Daniel winked at the penguin. "You ready, Jasper?"

The anatom nodded. Examining the discarded tubing, Jasper set about removing a communications receiver and attaching it to his neck. A bundle of his light-wire feathers extended down and plugged themselves into it.

Jasper cocked his head. Monitoring short-range Sinja communications, he wrote.

"Good."

Tau held out a small glass data chip to Ionica.

"What's this?" she asked when she took it.

"My father's sigil," said Tau. "Bantu Warriors will not answer your call without knowing who is asking for their help. If you can get a signal out."

Ionica nodded to thank him and tucked it into her utility belt.

Meanwhile, Daniel loaded Jasper into a backpack and threw the anatom over his shoulder. He looked Ionica squarely in the eye and said, "You ready?"

Nova held her sister back. "What are you about to do, Io?"

"You'll see," she replied.

Daniel made the long climb down the rope ladder hanging over the Barbatana's rear end, while from high up on the observation deck, Tau stuck two fingers into his mouth and whistled.

A herd of two-legged birdlike trabasaurs trotted over. Tau called them Yantis. Their shaggy brown feathers were missing in patches and their beaks sported long, needle-shaped teeth. They stank of something indescribable. Daniel tried not to get too much of a whiff as he hooked the reins of the nearest one and pulled himself into its saddle.

WHOMPFFFFFFFFFFFFFF!

From the back of the Barbatana, a blinding fireball suddenly launched into the air like a rocket, streaking higher and higher into the atmosphere until it looked like a wandering star.

Ionica was on her way.

Daniel adjusted the backpack. "You comfortable back there?"

Jasper hummed something cheerful in response.

"Okay." He jammed his feet into the stirrups and let out a loud *"Yah!"*

The Yanti shot across the landscape, heading for the Sinja stronghold.

Jasper, however, remained unsettled. Another holographic message popped up into Daniel's sights. How are we going to steal a ship? he asked.

"I don't know," Daniel said. "We'll figure it out when we get there."

36

FORTRESS OF LIES

Daniel and Jasper were about a mile outside of the fortress when the sky began to move.

Shadows flitted and darted around, circling the bright lights of the industrial compound like moths around a flame. But these were no moths.

These were Nightwatchers.

Daniel hadn't expected to ever see them again after he escaped the mines. He should have known better.

Mechanical man-sized insects, the Nightwatchers were the Sinja's preferred anatom watchdogs. And they were formidable. Sharp pincers and claws could snatch their prey and rip it into shreds within a couple of beats of their rubbery wings. Their vision could probe the darkness and pick out targets as though it were the brightest day. They showed no mercy. No compassion. No forgiveness.

Daniel brought the Yanti to a halt and jumped down. The powered armor adjusted to the lower gravity so that even though he'd used more energy than he should have, he didn't bounce. In fact, he could walk normally, which was a relief.

He fished the penguin out of his backpack and set him down. "Be careful. Nightwatchers don't hesitate. Remember: find me the easiest ship I can reach. Make sure it's fueled and ready to go. And make sure the security grid is down or we're not flying anywhere. Got that?"

Jasper raised a flipper in mock salute.

The Yanti bucked, trying not to trip over the anatom as he waddled between its legs.

Daniel thumbed a button on his utility belt. A holographic display popped up inside his helmet showing the route into the Sinja fortress.

"Comms check. Can you hear me?"

Jasper wrote back with a thumbs-up sign.

Daniel took a deep breath. What was he doing? Walking back into their clutches. This could all go horribly wrong. In fact, the odds were that this *would* all go wrong. But what choice did he have?

He set off across the moorland.

Soon after, the Yanti scarpered back to its herd, leaving behind an uneasy quiet. The night air whistled around Daniel's armor. He listened to the distant voices and the clank and creak of dwellings lashed to the backs of the Bar-batanas on their slow approach. They were far, far behind him and offered little in the way of protection, but still, for a moment, he thought about turning back.

No. He could still hear Vega Virrus in his head, telling him that he didn't matter.

It was not a lie Daniel was prepared to believe. He kept walking.

Soon, he passed through a series of outer fortifications. Early-warning systems for the most part. Their red lights pulsed brightly, but if they alerted anyone to Daniel's presence, they did so silently.

A little farther on, and a cohort of Overseers on patrol walked right in front of him, paying him no attention whatsoever.

Daniel's gut churned. To be so close to so many of them again—and to be alone. That creeping fear of being disappeared clawed at his neck and down his back.

He waited to be unmasked. Expected it. Didn't they know there was a traitor in their midst?

But they did not know. To them, he was simply another Mythrian soldier returning from a mission.

Daniel walked on, dread giving way to suffocating claustrophobia as the massive metal walls of the fortress towered in front of him, its gates wide open. Searchlights swept the landscape, the beams from static LightEyes that were stationed across the parapet.

Beyond, he saw the Sinja fleet, those massive ships from Musa Degh that had stolen his friends away. Would they know him if they saw him? Would he know them?

Everywhere he looked, Overseers marched while enginoids worked on heavy equipment, their bright welding arcs flashing against the night. The ships themselves stood on massive landing gear. They were connected to each other through airlock tubing, but they were only the first ring of this insane jumble of fortifications.

Behind them, interlocking BASE crawlers had been joined together to form what could only be described as a vast steel castle. Several platforms extended out from its walls, each holding a squadron of parked Phantoms, those dreadful Sinja starfighters. Towers lined the walls, each one bristling with cannons and other machines of war. And these were only the things Daniel recognized.

If this place's primary purpose was to instill fear, it worked. With every step, Daniel fought the urge to run the other way, an instinct that only got stronger when he stepped through the open gate and immediately regretted it.

"Who disturbs?" a familiar robotic voice wheezed.

A Nightwatcher swooped down to land in front of him. Tucking away its massive wings, its serrated metal talons plowed into the soil.

Daniel gasped. Wanted to flee, but stood paralyzed. The Nightwatcher regarded him, unblinking, while two more Nightwatchers joined the inspection.

Sweat beaded across Daniel's brow. Drops of salty

moisture stung his eyes. What was he supposed to do? Nova's Identifier should be working. They should know who he was, or at least who he was pretending to be.

With a gut full of acid, he forced himself to take a single faltering step forward, but the Nightwatchers blocked his way.

"Who disturbs?"

The first Nightwatcher clawed its way toward him, the ground crunching beneath its feet. It leaned right into his face as though sniffing the air.

Daniel didn't dare move. Couldn't move even if he wanted to. This shouldn't be happening. Why wasn't Nova's Identifier working?

The Nightwatcher grumbled; a strange, forlorn kind of confusion. "Who disturbs . . . ?"

Snap!

A flash of brilliant white lit up the inside of Daniel's helmet. Tiny arcs of static electricity sizzled around his scalp.

"Ouch!"

The Nightwatcher jerked its head back.

Daniel's socket rattled. Hummed. And then did what it was supposed to. It broadcast its response code.

Satisfied, the Nightwatchers didn't wait around. They stretched out their immense wings and shot off into the night sky.

Daniel's chest heaved. His legs wanted to give out. For a long while he still didn't want to move.

Eventually he thumbed his utility belt. "Okay, I'm in,"

he whispered with a gulp. "Which way?"

Jasper quickly updated the holographic map that Nova had given them from memory. Blinking arrows led the way. Daniel needed to get inside one of the ships. It was only by heading through their airlocked passages that he could enter the castle and begin to search for the Book of Planets.

"You have got to be kidding me," Daniel said, forcing himself onward. Each ship had to be half a mile long. Finding one with an open and accessible landing ramp could take forever. "You're monitoring their transmissions. Can't you patch into their systems and open up one of these doors?"

Jasper wrote back, Not programmed for magic.

"You could have fooled me."

Hissssssssssssssss!

Massive hydraulics slowly lowered a sturdy loading ramp down in front him. The clank of boots followed and a troop of Overseers soon emerged.

Daniel stepped politely to the side and waited for them to pass. The troop leader nodded to him as he went. "Your efforts in the relic war will be rewarded."

Daniel nodded back. "As will yours."

He waited until they were gone, then scurried up inside the ship before he lost his opportunity.

The ramp sealed shut behind him.

There was no going back now.

37

INFILTRATION

The vibrating deck plates pulsed beneath Daniel's boots.

The armor he wore felt less sluggish. More precise. Its power cells were recharging.

Good to know. Not that he expected to last more than a minute if a fight broke out, but he'd never be able to wear them down. All the more reason to stay out of trouble.

The loading deck was a hive of activity. There were stacks of cargo. Starfighters. And there were soldiers. Hundreds of them. Grubs he had once lived alongside who were now mind-controlled in Mythrian armor just like Nova had been. Some were marching away. Others were in combat training, their armor doing things he'd never seen before. Vents would open up revealing plasma jets that allowed them to unexpectedly dodge blows. Serrated fins would hook the legs of opponents.

Daniel made a note of everything he saw. If he ever got out of here, the Guild of Truth needed to know.

Okay, which way now? The map on Daniel's display told him he needed to reach the corridor on the other side—that led to the rear airlock.

Daniel tasted bile but made himself push on. What was the worst that could happen? Scratch that. The worst was obvious. The last thing he needed to do was will himself to fail.

Sticking to the outer edges of the loading deck, he made sure not to appear to be in a hurry. He stopped by a command console, pretending to check the readings. A soldier came up beside him. Pressed a few buttons. Moved on.

There was no small talk.

"I *knew* this was all a lie," Daniel whispered. "The legend said the Mythrian soldiers—via their armor—can see the future. That's what Tor Torin kept talking about. They relied on him thinking that."

In response, Jasper made a kind of cooing sound through the comms.

"They can't, or don't know how to, or they would have stopped me by now. I think that's why we haven't seen them in battle."

When there were no more consoles left to pretend to check, Daniel marched confidently toward the rear-facing corridor, right past a number of Mythrian soldiers who paid him no attention whatsoever, even as he made his way through the airlock and into the sprawling core of the facility.

The castle-like compound turned out to be hollow, just like a regular BASE crawler. All command centers were positioned around the perimeter, while at its center a series of crisscrossing gangways stretched across a chasm that exposed levels of the facility from top to bottom.

The only difference was the chronoscope, the dome-like structure he remembered from the mines. The one with the faces of the grubs in jars. The one where the Book of Planets was being kept. It sat far, far above him like some gigantic mechanical jellyfish. Miles of tubes and cables hung like tentacles from its underside, disappearing down into the bottomless chasm below.

There was only one way to reach the chronoscope: via the lifter nearby.

Stepping onto the platform, Daniel gripped the handrail and searched for the controls. There weren't any. What was he supposed to do now?

Suddenly, the lifter shuddered before rocketing up the side of the castle wall.

Someone had called for the elevator; the question was who.

"Jasper, did you do that?"

The anatom responded, No.

Daniel whispered into his comms, "Well, I'm heading up. Now would be a good time to figure out how to steal a ship. Where are you?"

No answer.

"Jasper?"

And then he saw him, a penguin waddling along right across from him on the far side of the facility, humming away to himself.

Jasper had paused to watch the occupants of a series of anatom breeding chambers. A fully grown squid-like corposum, the biological element of an anatom body, was being held suspended in a clear liquid and having its tentacles ripped off one by one. In turn, a robotic arm scooped up the severed tentacles and flushed them into adjacent chambers filled with some kind of growth medium. It didn't take long before they began swimming around like newborns, while the original corposum began to regrow its limbs.

Jasper visibly shuddered at the ghastly sight before moving on. But as he did so, he completely missed that just as he had been watching the corposum, the corposum had been watching him.

An anatom exosuit lowered into the breeding chamber for the corposum to climb into. The liquid flushed out. And when the chamber opened up, out scurried a very familiar-looking rodent.

Daniel couldn't believe it. "Hex!"

38

A DISSEMBLANCE OF SINJA

"Jasper," Daniel *warned. "Listen* to me. You're in danger. You're being followed."

If the penguin could hear him, he gave no obvious sign of it.

Hex A. Decimal, back in a rat suit. He'd know that anatom anywhere. First he stole the Book of Planets, and now he was following Jasper.

Daniel scratched around, seeing if he could stop the lifter, but there were no controls, and if he called out to warn him, both their covers would be blown.

He watched helplessly as Jasper called a lifter of his own down to a lower level, and Hex scuttled over to join him.

"Hey, pal. You're new. Mind if I tag along?" the rat said to the penguin in Mendese.

Hearing that familiar click language through his comms was unsettling at best. "Don't trust him," Daniel urged.

Jasper, meanwhile, simply looked the rat up and down. Then hummed.

Hex nodded. "Sure, I can help you find that. I love making new friends."

Daniel wanted to scream.

Chudder-chumm.

The lifter jerked to a stop at chronoscope level one.

The gangway sat empty, overshadowed by a much wider and busier walkway above it. Daniel ducked out before he ended up being whisked to that level instead.

The clank of boots marched back and forth above his head. He peered up between the deck plates. An entire squad of Mythrian soldiers lined the route into the chronoscope. A figure in black rags swept between them—Vega Virrus had returned. A Mythrian commander strode with him. He wasn't wearing a helmet. He wore the colored sash of a trusted aide and true believer.

Blink Darkada.

Daniel's heart sank. There was his old friend, promoted and powerful. From slave to officer, content with his choice to live with the darkness.

"Vega Seftis has convened the entire Dissembly," Blink announced, stiff and awkward.

"Make sure I am not disturbed," Virrus whispered in reply.

Blink nodded, turned back, and signaled to someone. Daniel couldn't see who or where. Within moments, every door into the chronoscope began to roll shut.

Daniel sprinted down the gangway and ducked inside before the exit sealed with a hiss.

He stood by the locked door for a moment, unwilling to move. It was so dark in here he could barely see. The room hummed with electricity, and somewhere in the gloom something was scuttling about.

When his eyes adjusted sufficiently he pushed on.

Plink-plink-plink.

One by one, clusters of eerie faces shone brightly, each one sealed in a clear vial. They peered at him, trapped and afraid. Daniel knew these faces. He had seen them before. The disembodied copies of every grub he had ever known in the mines and beyond.

His own face had once been here, until he smashed it. He'd had no idea of what he had been destroying in his bid to escape the mines. Fear had taken control and made him act.

Now he had questions.

What possible purpose did this machine serve?

"Ah, Vega Virrus," an unfamiliar voice announced, each syllable dripping with disdain. "So good of you to join us."

"I had matters to attend to," Virrus hissed back.

Daniel shot a look high up at the ceiling. He was under the floor of a conference room. Through the slits in the deck plates he could just make out figures standing around a command console—a council of the most feared Sinja in the galaxy.

Daniel froze. If he could see *them*, it wouldn't be long before they noticed *him*. With the exception of Virrus, they sparkled briefly every so often, revealing that they were holocule avatars connected to their owners through the communications system. As Daniel was acutely aware, unlike holograms, holocules allowed the user to see what was in the room where they stood.

"Juba is ours," Virrus announced.

"Juba is *mine*," the first speaker corrected.

The bottom fell out of Daniel's stomach. If Juba had fallen, what had become of Ionica's family?

"I would say that Juba is *his*," another speaker whispered. "Virrus has done more to bring this plan to fruition than you have, Seftis."

Seftis? Vega Seftis himself? When the Book of Planets had been stolen—it felt so long ago now—Daniel remembered the name Seftis being mentioned at every emergency meeting he had attended, both in the Forum, and privately with the Guardians of Truth in Tor Torin's chambers.

They called him the Lord of Lies. Merely uttering his name seemed to offend some Truth Seekers. Though ordinary Sinja turned on each other as much as they turned on Truth Seekers, Vega Seftis seemed to be the one Sinja they all bowed before.

Daniel squeezed between the clusters of tubes, trying to get a look at this Lord of Lies for himself, but it was impossible; all he could see were feet.

"Vega Malice," Seftis hissed. "I would be pleased to add your mask to my collection."

"I meant no insult," Malice mused.

"Remind me what you have brought to this endeavor."

Vega Malice. That was a new one. Daniel hadn't heard of this Sinja before.

"Darius Hun has made contact with the Achorint," Malice replied confidently. "He has delivered the Klithi, and I will have control of Felonis soon."

Daniel had no idea what the Klithi was, but the Achorint? That was another name Tor Torin had mentioned before. Some mad scientist with no moral compass. And Darius Hun—he was the criminal the Truth Seekers had been pursuing when they boarded the cargo ship *WaKeenee* and saved Daniel's life.

Daniel had watched Hun's trial, watched him rave about the war to come.

This war.

Hun had relished the idea of being exiled to Felonis, the prison planet. Because that had been the plan all along.

Nova was right. The chaos *was* a distraction. The Sinja had set deeper plans in motion long before Daniel's escape. But what were those plans really? So many names. So many pieces of the puzzle. Seftis, Malice, Darius Hun, and now this scientist the Achorint again. Daniel *had* to get this information back to Tor Torin.

A cluster of luminous tubes shoved Daniel aside. The chronoscope was rearranging the tubes; for what purpose Daniel could not imagine. Daniel moved out of the way until one face amid one particular tree of faces stood out. It sat inside a sickly tube that flickered as tiny mechanical bugs crawled all over it, attempting to fix the problem.

The face inside was Nova's.

Daniel approached slowly and reached out to grasp the holocule container. Sensing his presence, the tiny bugbots pulled back to allow him access.

It made sense. He was wearing Nova's Identifier, but he had removed the helmet umbilical. As far as they were concerned, Nova still existed, but they—*they couldn't control her.*

Is that what this machine did? Was *this* how they controlled the grubs?

Daniel snatched Nova's tube and clipped it to his utility belt.

The bugbots chattered among themselves, alarmed and not quite sure how to proceed—

"Then consult the Book of Planets and *find me a candidate!*" Seftis roared from the room above. "We need the Twelve. Not the six. Not the eight."

What had begun as simmering resentment had turned into a full-blown argument.

"These artifacts are millions of years old!" another Sinja shot back. "Did it ever occur to you that some may have been destroyed? One could easily have fallen into a black hole, or been disintegrated by a supernova—"

"To destroy one is to destroy them all," Seftis replied, seething. "The others are out there."

"This plan is foolish," another Sinja spat. "You have asked us to jeopardize our bases of power on this single fantasy, and for what? I am withdrawing from this Dissembly."

The room above fell silent as the holocule of an angry Sinja fizzled out.

"That's it?" Vega Malice remarked. "We just allow her to walk away?"

"Vega Putra will be dealt with," Seftis replied evenly. "Virrus, bring the book."

Daniel listened to the sound of controls being activated. And then, at the heart of the chamber where he stood, just beyond more clusters of illuminated glass vials, a shaft of light suddenly lanced up from a hole in the deck.

The Book of Planets levitated up from its hiding place, and rose toward the room above.

Daniel's tongue caught in his throat. There it was— within his grasp. For one brief moment he stood bolted to the ground, unsure of what he should do.

A hatch began dilating into the room above.

Now was his chance!

Daniel bolted for the Book of Planets, forcing his way through the eerie clusters of holocule grub faces.

He leapt into the shaft of light, his arms outstretched.

His armored fingers clenched the book with both hands.

But his momentum did not carry him through to the other side.

Instead, Daniel found himself trapped in the beam of light with the book, levitating up into the presence of the gathered Sinja.

Soon he was standing on the command console in front of them all, the Book of Planets held tightly in his hands.

Oops.

"Hi," Daniel said, searching for the exit.

And then he saw him.

Vega Seftis, the Lord of Lies himself. His mask a grotesque mishmash of other masks, sewn roughly together so that the faces of his enemies were melded into one hideous visage.

"Who is this?" Seftis demanded.

Daniel gathered his courage. "I am ex-prisoner forty-one eighty-two," he said. "Seeker of Truth. Keeper of the Book of Planets. And denier of your power."

He yanked his helmet off so that everyone in the room could see exactly who he was. "I am Daniel Coldstar," he said, and tossed the helmet at Virrus.

Instinctively, the Sinja caught it, giving Daniel just enough time to leap from the console, hammer the controls to one of the doors, and wave.

"Bye!" he said. And he was gone.

39

GOING SO SOON?

Klaxons shrieked throughout the Sinja compound.

AH-OOOO-HA! AH-OOOO-HA! AH-OOOO-HA!

Outside the chronoscope, Daniel tucked the Book of Planets under his arm and barreled down the walkway, running headlong at a troop of Mythrian soldiers who stood their ground and fired back.

Pew! Pew! Pew! Pew! Pew!

Daniel dove over the side of the walkway, reached out with his free hand, and swung himself down into the gangway below.

"Jasper!" he cried, bringing up the holographic console projected from his utility belt. "We gotta go!"

A melodic tune chirped back through the commlink.

"Just point the way," Daniel added, racing along the

gangway while his map updated—

Slam!

A pair of boots plowed into Daniel's back, knocking him flying.

He skittered across the deck, barely holding on to the book as he went.

Daniel twisted around.

Blink Darkada stood barely six paces behind him. His pale eyes seemed haunted. What had he seen? What had he regretted? What was he thinking, seeing Daniel now after so much time?

"It's good to see you," Daniel said, pulling himself up onto his feet.

Blink stared at him as though he were figuring out the quickest way to kill his prey.

"I miss my friend," Daniel said.

"We're not friends." Blink took a step forward.

Instinctively, Daniel pulled his arm back to ready his Aegis—

Nothing happened. Blast it, he didn't *have* his Aegis!

Though he did have something more powerful. "I know your real name," he said.

Blink stopped in his tracks.

"You're a liar."

Daniel shrugged. "I can't lie. I'm a Truth Seeker." He took a step back, his eyes searching for an escape route. "I know where you're from too."

"You know nothing."

Daniel lifted his chin. "You are Kardas Darkada of Kith. Your mother is Laleh. I met her. I know she *loves* you and wants you *home*."

Laleh's words echoed in Daniel's ears. Blink wouldn't do this.

Daniel backed up again. "I know you're trapped. I know you had some kind of plan and you can't get out of it. But come with me and we can leave now! Together!"

He had no idea if any of that was true, but if it reached a part of Blink's soul, it had to be worth it.

Blink held his hand out. "Give me the book."

"I can't do that, Blink. You're going to have to take it from me."

"If you insist."

Blink came at him, but Daniel was quicker. He rolled under the handrail and tumbled over the edge, pulling almost the same trick that he had before. He dangled from the girders beneath the gangway, looking for somewhere to land.

Pew! Pew! Pew! Pew! Pew!

Energy bolts crisscrossed at him from all angles.

"Someone had to lead you out of those mines!" Blink yelled at him from above. "You really thought you were smart enough to figure it out on your own?"

"I know you're lying," Daniel called back.

Over there, he saw another gangway. It was several

floors down, but if he got the angle right, in this lower gravity, he might just make it. Daniel started swinging back and forth.

"I was never your friend, Daniel Coldstar!" Blink roared. "I was your prison guard!"

The word stung with the power that only lies carried.

"I don't believe you," Daniel said, then released his grip.

He shot out into the chasm, following one gigantic arc toward his target. The gangway raced up at him—

Slam!

Daniel hit the deck far harder than he had expected. The Book of Planets flew out of his arms and skidded along the deck plates.

Clank!

It slammed into Blink Darkada's boots just as he landed on the same deck.

Daniel pulled himself up and charged at Blink in the hopes he could reach the book before he had time to react.

But it was too late; Blink flicked the book over the edge with his toe.

"No!" Daniel cried.

The Book of Planets tumbled end over end, landing with an almighty clank. Daniel didn't have time to see where it went. He balled his fist and swung at Blink.

The Mythrian armor sensed his movements and increased power, plowing Daniel's fist into Blink's chest.

Blink skidded back, then balled his own fists and rained

down blow after ferocious blow.

Daniel blocked. Threw another punch, following it with his forearm.

Blink smashed it.

Daniel twisted and kicked him in the gut.

He glanced over the guardrail, searching for the book. Where did it go? Everything was so dark down there.

Slam!

Daniel wheezed, the air knocked out of him as Blink jabbed a punch right into his back. He collapsed to his knees.

Slam! Slam!

Blink hammered him mercilessly, then flipped him over, pummeled his chest.

Daniel sobbed in agony. He tried fighting back, but he just didn't have the strength. He threw up his arms to protect his face, only to have Blink bear down on him, forcing his arms away.

He grabbed Daniel by the throat and leaned in close.

Terror struck Daniel. He shook, fully expecting to die.

And then Blink whispered, "I know how to defeat them."

Daniel tried to respond but nothing came out.

"Don't react, they're watching," he whispered. "They watch everything. Why are you here? Are you alone?"

Was this a trick? Was this real? Daniel couldn't tell anymore.

"Ships from three different worlds are about to pound

this base into sand," he whispered back, hoping that what he was saying had some truth to it.

Blink actually looked relieved. "Good," he said. For the briefest moment, real emotion washed over his face. "It took me a long time to figure it out. I wish I'd figured it out sooner, but I wasn't smart enough. If I had, this all could have ended a long time ago. I'm sorry."

Stunned, Daniel barely knew how to respond. "What are you talking about?"

"I know how to free everyone," Blink said. "Now punch me. Fight me off. They can't suspect—"

Daniel gladly smashed him in the face.

Blink rolled away as . . .

Schhhhhweeeee . . .

The screaming sound of engines drew closer. What were they going to do, blast him to pieces with heavy-weapons fire? There had to be somewhere he could go.

Slam! Smash!

Blink threw punch after punch until—

Craaackkkkkkkkkkkkk!

The walkway shuddered and screamed, then cracked apart. The nose of a screaming Phantom starfighter pitched up through the wreckage, forcing the two boys apart.

Through the cockpit glass, Daniel spied a penguin at the controls, and he had the Book of Planets with him.

"Look for the signal!" Blink hollered, trying to stay on his feet and not get blown away.

"What signal?"

"You'll know it when you see it!"

Daniel shook, trying not to weep. Trying not to get sucked into yet another deception. "How do I know you're telling the truth, Blink?"

Blink smiled. "You always did have good instincts, Dee. I'll see you around."

And with that, weapons fire erupted again. Daniel leapt onto the Phantom's wing and threw the cockpit hatch open.

"Let's go!" he cried, climbing inside.

Jasper, humming merrily to himself, threw the Phantom into overdrive and rocketed up, firing at anything that got in their way.

"I don't understand what just happened," Daniel said, breathless. He felt sick to his stomach.

From somewhere in the rear of the cockpit, a familiar voice speaking clicking Mendese said, "You pulled off a miracle, that's what happened, kid."

The voice belonged to Hex.

40

MASSIF ATTACK

Hex A. Decimal sat inside a cage, his arms tied to the bars.

His chest was open and wires had been plunged into the pale white corposum and plugged into the Phantom's computer.

Daniel called back over his shoulder. "What's *he* doing here?" he demanded.

"Hey, kid. Glad to see a friendly face. How you been?" Hex said.

"I was talking to Jasper," Daniel snapped.

He climbed up and peered over the pilot's seat. Jasper pushed forward on the attitude controls. The Sinja Phantom rocketed upward, rolling from side to side, dodging the crossfire. "Well?"

Jasper stretched his neck out and glanced back,

wondering what the problem was. He flipped a control to activate a dialogue box on the heads-up display.

Need him, Jasper said.

Incredulous, Daniel shot back, "Need him *how*? Nobody needs that traitor."

He has the security codes, Jasper explained. Now we have them too.

"You'll never escape," Hex commented. "You know that, right, kid?"

Jasper tapped away on the starfighter's controls. The wires sticking out of Hex lit up. Outside, a hole in the security grid big enough to fly through rolled open.

The Phantom burst out into Massif's night sky, swooping around to fire on the nearest tower. Searchlights skimmed its hull. Ground fire erupted.

"Never escape, huh?" Daniel sneered. He reached over and grabbed the Book of Planets. "Like we were never going to get *this* back?" he said. "You started a war across the galaxy. You caused the deaths of I don't know how many people."

Hex tried to shrug it off. "I was programmed to get that."

"Like you were programmed to betray me too?" Daniel said, tucking the book away.

"Yes! That's exactly what I was programmed to do. It's not personal."

"It's personal *to me*," Daniel growled. Climbing over into the pilot's seat, he nudged Jasper. "Get out of the chair."

Jasper dutifully relinquished the controls.

"I was *programmed* to betray you, kid," Hex explained. "When your friend here asked for help, there was nothing to stop me from helping *him*. It was the least I could do."

"Oh, you're tied up in a cage by choice?" Daniel shook his head. "Jasper, figure out a way to shut him up, or I'm opening the hatch and dumping him out into space right now."

"You do what you gotta do, kid," Hex said.

Jasper shrieked. Daniel took the warning, hit the flight stick, and hoped for the best.

Outside, a gigantic Barbatana collapsed under the onslaught of relentless Sinja weapons fire. Jasper maneuvered the Phantom around its lolling head, as it tumbled to one side, flipped the village tied to its back, and flung the villagers out.

"Since when do you know how to fly?" Hex wondered.

Daniel ignored him. He banked the ship around so he could see out the cockpit glass. The train of Barbatanas had arrived at the Sinja compound, just as Nova and Tau had promised—and the diversion had begun.

The massive trabasaurs stomped on the Sinja defenses, destroying and crushing every last placement they could find. Overseers and Mythrian soldiers scattered to avoid their ultimate obliteration, exchanging fire with the Massif warriors firing blaser cannons from the backs of their gargantuan mounts.

Daniel checked the comms channels. "Long-range comms are back online!" He thumbed a channel. "Ionica, do you read me? Ionica, do you read me?"

By the Fuse, he hoped she was out there somewhere.

"Ionica, please respond."

Nothing.

He banked the Phantom around, only to have the alert system explode into a frenzy. Sinja attack ships began popping up on the targeting display on the inside of the cockpit glass.

Bleep! Bleep! Bleep!

Phantoms coming right at us! Jasper announced.

"Jasper, man the secondary weapons and deploy the decoys!" Daniel barked.

On it.

Outside, exact holecule copies of their Phantom starfighter began spawning and peeling off, drawing some of the ground fire away.

"Hold on!" Daniel warned. He punched the controls, and the Phantom rocketed up into the sky at maximum velocity, pushing everyone back in their seats.

Jasper fired up the controls on the rear console and began unloading on the tailing fighters.

Blam! Blam!

The Phantom rocked as incoming fire seared the ship's hull.

Daniel thumbed the long-range communications.

"This is Truth Seeker Daniel Coldstar! To all friendly vessels, Massif has been invaded. I repeat—Sinja forces have taken Massif. There is no quarantine! The House Soto requests immediate assistance! We are under attack!"

He didn't have the sigil but it would hopefully be enough to get someone to respond.

KA-BOOM!

Heavy cannons exploded in massive fireballs.

Blam! Blam! Blam!

The Phantom rocked wildly.

"Gee, a real shame this is all going to end so badly," Hex lamented. "And I liked you, too."

Daniel gritted his teeth and ignored him.

Da-ding-da-ding-da-ding!

Jasper pounded on the rear controls. We're losing an engine!

Daniel started scratching around the flight controls, hitting switches seemingly at random.

SSHHHHHHHHHHHHHMMMMMMMMMMMMM!

"What the heck are you doing, kid? Those are the air brakes!" Hex declared, his Mendese clicks way louder and angrier than most people ever got to hear.

"What's the matter? You sound afraid," Daniel snapped back.

The trailing attack ships raced past, giving Daniel just enough time to alter his trajectory and hit the throttle–heading straight back down for the Sinja base.

Why are we going back? Jasper asked with alarm.

"Blink said I had to wait for the signal."

What signal?

"I don't know! He said I'd know it when I saw it."

Hex chortled. "You still have faith in your friend. Cute, kid."

Racing through the night air, Daniel nosed the starfighter up and banked hard, circling the battle below, trying to figure out whatever this signal was supposed to be.

Blam! Blam! Blam!

More ground fire. More Sinja starfighters attacking from all angles.

What do we do when we see the signal? said Jasper.

Oh no, that was a really good question. Daniel hadn't thought about it. What was he supposed to do?

And then, the most unexpected of signals rose up from the center of the Sinja fortress. The chronoscope lit up ghostly green and began its slow rise into Massif's night air. Hatches opened in its sides and glittering debris began raining down on the base below.

The holocule tubes were being jettisoned, cascading down like a waterfall.

When he'd first escaped the mines, so long ago now, he had found his own holocule tube and smashed it. He hadn't realized it until today, but that very act had prevented the

Sinja from ever regaining control over him. What's more—
Blink had seen him do it.

Now the very things that controlled every other grub
out there were vulnerable.

Daniel knew exactly what to do.

"That's it!" he roared.

He jerked on the yoke, yanking the ship onto a new
course, and flew at the diabolical contraption as fast as the
ship's one remaining engine would carry them.

He hammered on the trigger, firing the main cannons
and lighting up the chronoscope, reducing it to fireballs
within fireballs.

The mechanical jellyfish lurched and heaved, before
breaking apart, its tentacles yanked from its obscene body,
its fiery innards exploding and raining down debris on the
Sinja below.

KKKKKAAAABBOOOOOOOOOMMMMMMMMM!

All Sinja thought control fell silent.

Almost immediately the ground fire ceased.

Daniel cut the throttle, bringing the Phantom down to
a crawl.

He sat back in the pilot's seat and took a well-earned
breath.

Jasper, however, watched the scene unfolding outside.
Checking and rechecking the readings on his console, he
gestured outside. Look, he messaged.

Daniel pushed himself up to the cockpit glass. "What is it?"

Down below, amid the wreckage of the Sinja fortress, hundreds, perhaps thousands of Mythrian soldiers were emerging from their ships in something of a daze. Here and there they began taking their helmets off and casting them aside.

They breathed the air as though breathing it for the first time.

For a moment, it appeared as though they had not even noticed the hordes of Overseers rushing at them, their blast-pikes sparking, intent on rounding them up and regaining control. But the grubs were in no mood to be rounded up. They had been trained as Mythrian soldiers, after all, and they were still wearing that ancient power armor.

The Overseers never knew what hit them when the revolution began.

"They're free!" Daniel laughed, tears in his eyes, watching the revolt unfold. "Blink did it! They're free!"

But that was not what Jasper had been trying to warn him about. He tapped him on the shoulder and directed him to look out the other side of the cockpit window.

In another part of the fortress, Blink Darkada was fighting for his life against the wrath of Vega Virrus.

"No," Daniel yelped. "No, no!" He threw himself at the flight controls, working the switches blindly. "How do we land this thing? How do we land?"

A ring of Overseers had penned Blink in. Virrus attacked, the tendrils of his cloak snapping Blink's legs out from under him. They grabbed him by the ankles, raised him up, and smashed him against any hard surface they could find.

Blink did not cry out.

He gritted his teeth and took the blows, but his armor had started to give out. Sparks arced out of the joints, casings flew off.

Blood spilled.

Daniel grabbed the yoke and spun the Phantom around, trying to take aim at Virrus. When the targeting system bleeped, he unleashed what he had, but Virrus was too wily and too fast. He leapt through the air, dragging Blink with him, directly into the line of fire.

Daniel cut the trigger and blew the cockpit.

Launching himself out of the craft, he crashed the last few feet to the ground just as Vega Virrus powered up his Askarai, the Sinja variant of a Truth Seeker's Aegis, and pummeled the boy between two huge boulders.

There was an almighty crunch.

And Blink Darkada dropped to the ground.

"No!" Daniel roared, tears and rage and spittle flying from his mouth. "No! No! No!"

Virrus fled, his Overseers fleeing with him.

"I WILL HUNT YOU!" Daniel raged. "I WILL FIND YOU!"

He ran to his friend and dropped to his knees, convulsing in tears. He wiped the blood from Blink's face and cradled him. He rocked him back and forth, but no amount of comfort would bring him back.

And when Jasper eventually joined him, his chest heaved and he just kept saying, "I think he's asleep. I think he's going to be okay."

And he knew it was the biggest lie he'd ever told anyone.

And even though the night sky was now filled with flashes of white, bringing ships from all over the galaxy to battle the retreating remains of the Sinja fleet; and even though the sound of Ionica Lux's voice on an open channel letting him know that she was safe and had brought help should have brought him joy, Daniel couldn't find it in himself to embrace it.

Instead he held his friend. And stroked his hair.

And said good-bye to him.

41

HOMECOMING

"Sinja vessel. Stay on your assigned flight path or you will be fired upon," the pilot in the Truth Seeker Spitfire announced.

"Understood," Daniel replied, watching the squadron of Truth Seeker starfighters escort them down to the landing site on Orpheus Core.

It had been hours since the battle on Massif. Daniel, drained and verging on collapse, didn't have a tear left in him.

"I don't know why you brought me here," Hex said from his makeshift prison, watching the old familiar landscape streak by. "There are plenty of places you could have dropped me off. Let bygones be bygones, you know?"

"Nah," Daniel replied easily. "A lot of people down there

are itching to see you."

"That's what I'm afraid of."

Jasper triggered the maneuvering thrusters and brought the starfighter in for its landing. The ship hovered for a moment before gently setting down on the hardtop on the outskirts of the Fortress of Truth, opposite the *Equinox*.

A security detail of Truth Watchmen were waiting for them. But beyond the pad, a crowd of Truth Seekers were gathering, many of them running to see what was going on.

Daniel popped the hatch without waiting for the engines to finish cycling down.

He poked his head out before standing up, and then quietly made his way down, clutching the Book of Planets.

From the landing ramp of the *Equinox*, he watched Tor Torin make his way down to greet him. The diminutive Keeper of Truth seemed hunched with worry and looked closer to his real age than ever before.

He stood in front of Daniel and watched him through dark eyes brimming with concern and compassion.

"I see you brought the body," Tor Torin said. "He will have an honorable burial."

Daniel nodded, handing him the Book of Planets in silence.

Torin held the weighty metal tome in his hand with reverence. "I thought we would never see this again," he said. "I had rather hoped we wouldn't. But I don't know what would happen to the universe if we destroyed it."

A flicker of a smile touched his lips.

Daniel tried returning the favor.

"And that is a *very* interesting outfit you're wearing."

"This old Mythrian armor? Don't worry, it's yours. I know you're eager to rip it apart and study it."

"Yes, but not with you in it."

Daniel nodded to the Truth Watchmen. "Please place that rat in the ship under arrest," he said.

Jasper pushed the cage up out of the cockpit with Hex still in it and shoved it over the edge. It landed on the ground with a crunch. "Hey, you can't do this!" Hex yelled.

"I can and I have," Daniel said, as the Watchmen hauled the cage away. "Everyone answers for their crimes, Hex. Even you—"

"Come," Torin said, tucking the Book of Planets under his arm. "I'm afraid we have much to discuss before this day is over. Let's get you cleaned up, fed, and watered."

"I failed," Daniel said.

"If by 'failed,' you mean you freed five thousand seven hundred and twenty-six coerced hostages," he said, "then yes. I'd say you failed spectacularly."

"But Blink's gone," Daniel whispered.

"Yes," Torin said, resting a hand on Daniel's shoulder. "Yes, he is."

42

THE TWELVE

In Torin's chambers a little while later, Daniel, Ionica, and Nova waited while a council of senior Truth Guardians and officers of the War Guild quietly filed out, clearly disturbed by the briefing they had just received.

In the middle of the room sat a hologram of Juba.

"I've had a chance to peruse your father's research," Torin declared, talking directly to the two girls. "I'm afraid you're in for a bit of a surprise," he said.

Torin turned his attention to the hologram.

"Juba isn't real," he said.

Daniel struggled to understand. "Seemed real to me."

"Not a real planet," Torin explained. "It's hollow. Artificial. The entire thing was constructed by the Destronomers and then *disguised* as a planet. Its mountains were created, its rivers predetermined. But fundamentally, Juba is a relic. Albeit an extraordinarily large one, but a relic nonetheless."

Nova was aghast. "What does it do?"

"I was hoping you could tell us, but alas, you don't seem to possess that knowledge."

Daniel wandered over for a better look at the hologram. "The Sinja Dissembly said that it was one of the Twelve. They said Massif and Felonis were ones too?"

"Yes," Torin agreed. "We took a few readings and it does seem that Massif is an artificial planet too. Felonis, well, that's another story. We're never going to be granted the authority to study such a busy prison planet, but it does give one pause."

"How so?" Ionica said.

"Because that is where this mad Sinja scientist, the Achorint, is imprisoned. And what with this new information coming to light about Darius Hun getting himself caught on purpose, specifically to meet him there, I'd say there's a high probability that it is indeed the case that Felonis is also a relic and they're up to something."

Torin wandered back to his favorite chair and sat down. "I just don't know what good it will do him. It's not like he's ever going to be able to escape."

"Famous last words," Nova warned.

"Quite."

"But what does the Achorint think is going to happen when he finds these twelve planet-sized relics?" Daniel wondered.

"I don't know," Torin said. "But what worries me more is what Vega Seftis thinks he is going to do with all of this power."

"How do we stop him?" Daniel asked.

A twinkle danced in Tor Torin's eyes. "The Sinja suffered a massive defeat today. We won this battle. Enjoy the moment, Daniel, because there will be more battles to come. And for those," he said, "rest assured, I have a plan."

43

ORDER OF AXIOM

Blink Darkada was laid to rest in the Garden of Heroes and given full Truth Seeker honors—for his actions, they had treated him as one of their own.

In time, Daniel returned to his studies at the Guild of Truth. With his sleeks polished and bright, his Aegis back where it was meant to be, life, at least from the outside, appeared to return to normal. Though it could never truly be. Daniel had seen too much, experienced too much—lost too much—for his life ever to be truly normal.

He remained restless, and after a while, his senses told him that he had been correct to feel that way. Something wasn't quite right. He couldn't put his finger on it, but as the days passed he got the distinct impression that there was going to be a reckoning. He had placed so many people in danger with his actions that he started getting the sense that his days as a Truth Seeker were numbered.

Perhaps it was for the best.

The feeling first started in Zubenel Genubi's class, when the geriatric Truth Guardian suddenly started treating him differently. Not badly. Just differently. And from there the feeling grew.

Then Ionica grew distant, though she *was* spending a great deal of time with her sister. With Juba still in turmoil, her entire family had relocated to one of the temporary refugee camps, and she seemed delighted to have them so close by. But then when Ben started doing it and Astrid— that's when he knew.

They were going to ask him to leave the Guild.

So when the summons to attend a hearing at the Forum was presented to him, Daniel was not in the least bit surprised.

He put on his sleeks and held his head high and quietly let himself in through the witness entrance and waited with the Sergeant-at-Arms, while Tor Torin continued to give his impassioned speech out on the dais in front of a packed auditorium.

"And that is our dilemma," Torin said. "That is our burden to bear as Truth Seekers. When we know that there are so many lies, do we spend our energies fact-checking each and every one, knowing that lies can be generated faster than we can prove that they are so? Or do we act more judiciously? Do we strike at the heart of the lie machine itself and cut off the source?"

He paused to let the audience absorb that idea.

"And then what do we do with the people who believed them? Force them to look at the truth and they will deny it. You cannot force the truth on someone. When they are lost, they are lost. They refuse all help. Our duty is to present the truth and facts as plainly as possible. Be at peace. The burden of frustration is not yours to carry. Lift it from your shoulders. They cannot see what they cannot see. It is not your responsibility to get them to see the truth. It is theirs. They will be angry. They will fight, they will react. And the deeper the truth, the more they will react, because some part of them, somewhere deep, deep down, has recognized that truth and is wrestling with it from within."

It was weird coming into the room in the middle of a speech.

Daniel glanced up at the Sergeant-at-Arms. "What the heck is this about? You're just stripping me of my Aegis and kicking me out of the Guild, right?" he whispered. "What's with the weird speech?"

Suddenly, he realized that Tor Torin was summoning him in an overly formal manner. "The Guild of Truth calls Beacon Daniel Coldstar!"

"I think he means you," the Sergeant-at-Arms said softly.

Unsure of what he was about to face, Daniel stepped from the wings and joined Torin on the dais.

The Forum was packed to capacity. He saw Ben in the audience first. Then Ionica and Nova. He saw Astrid and he saw Nails, Fix, and Rann. Their faces were inscrutable.

Everyone was staring at him. It made his skin itch.

"Do you know why you're here, Daniel?" Torin asked gently.

"I think so."

"Would it surprise you to learn that this gathering is being broadcast to the entire galaxy?"

That didn't make sense. "Why?"

"Look into the audience. Who do you see?"

Daniel didn't know how to respond. "Friends," he said with a shrug. "Beacons." He kept glancing around at all the new faces. What was he supposed to see? Everyone he'd put in danger? Was he supposed to apologize?

And why was that boy grinning at him? And that one too?

Wait a minute. He knew these faces. He'd lived with these faces. He'd suffered and survived in the mines with these faces. These were his fellow grubs. He knew them. How he knew them! Ogle Cog and Dakan Liss, the list went on and on—they were here, *and they were free*!

Daniel gulped.

Torin rested a proud hand on his shoulder when he saw the flicker of recognition. "These are the ones you saved, Daniel," he said. "Five thousand seven hundred and twenty-six souls. But you didn't just save *them*. You saved their families too. Families who no longer have to bear the torment of wondering what happened to their children. Four thousand nine hundred and eighty-five mothers, four thousand one hundred and twenty-two fathers, twenty-six thousand five hundred and three siblings—all no longer live under the merciless oppression of the Sinja. And we are broadcasting this because we know that there are other parents out there, and we pledge to them that we will find their children, and that they no longer need to be afraid.

"You did this, Daniel. You did this."

"But I didn't. What about Blink? I didn't do this alone."

"No one ever does," said Torin, stepping back. "Sergeant Keep, you may proceed."

The Sergeant-at-Arms did not reply directly. Instead, he announced, "All rise! All rise!"

Once the audience was on their feet, he produced a holographic scroll and rolled it open, close enough to read.

"For bravery, above and beyond that required of a Beacon! For services to the Guild of Truth, and in the pursuit of Truth! I, Cygnus Keep, Sergeant-at-Arms, on behalf of a thankful galaxy, do hereby present Beacon Daniel Coldstar with the Order of Axiom!"

The Sergeant-at-Arms turned to Daniel and affixed a bronze hexagon to Daniel's chest. The medal melted into his sleeks, becoming a permanent part of his uniform. A moment later, a bronze stripe ran down his right arm from shoulder to cuff.

Sergeant Keep shook his hand and smiled. "Well done, son."

Daniel went to speak, but no words came out. His lips trembled.

The entire auditorium burst into applause. Cheers erupted from the highest balconies. Amid so many joyful faces, he even found Tor Torin beaming at him.

For a moment, he didn't know what to do. Humbly, he took a step forward toward the audience and listened to their cheers.

And after a moment—Daniel Coldstar smiled.

GLOSSARY

The following entries have been retrieved from the *Encyclopedia Exodussica, 10th Edition*.

AIR-DRIVE: Air-Drives are personal vehicles used by the vast majority of citizens across all galactic star nations. They range in size from single-seater Bullets and two-seater Clodhoppers to large recreational Momes. Air-Drives are generally used at ground level, but are capable of short hops into and out of orbit in order to dock with faster-than-light-equipped vessels for journeys to other star systems.
VOL. 100.588

AZUL FLATS: The Azul Flats are a Galactic Park of Distinction situated on the dayside of the planet Juba, which is renowned for its blue lava. The name of the lava is actually a misnomer, since the glowing blue color is due to the combustion of unusually high concentrations of sulfuric gases at very high temperatures. The first incidence of blue lava recorded in human history was reported at the Kawah Ijen volcano, Indonesia, on Earth.

VOL. 231.900

BANTU WORLDS: The Bantu Worlds are a wealthy and powerful star nation originally settled by colonists from ancient Earth's African continent. The Bantu Worlds have a distinct culture and language that prefers to remain separate and distinct from other human civilizations throughout the galaxy, prompted by their mistreatment at the hands of other human cultures in antiquity. Citizens of some Bantu Worlds can be suspicious of visitors.

VOL. 341.382

BARBATANA: *Barbatana titanis trabasauri* are the largest known trabasaurs in the galaxy. Their genetic code is designed to allow Barbatanas to adapt to their environment at birth, rather than relying on evolutionary adaption over several generations. Barbatanas serve an agricultural function, producing enormous quantities of nitrogen-rich fertilizer.

VOL. 499.596

BASE CRAWLER: Battle Armored Sentry Enclosures, or BASE crawlers, are massive armored vehicles designed to secure the beachhead when landing military forces on an enemy planet. BASE crawlers are usually several stories high and superficially resemble spiders or scorpions when spotted at a distance. Eight powerful legs transport the vehicle, for maximum stability. When BASE crawlers reach their target, the entire body detaches and lands on the ground to serve as a tactical command post. The eight legs burrow into the ground and their upper armor is jettisoned, transforming them into defensive cannon towers.

VOL. 584.879

COLDSTAR: The SL *Coldstar* was a passenger starliner owned and operated by the civilian cruise ship corporation the Neutron Star Line. In EE 9291, the *Coldstar* was attacked by unknown assailants while cruising toward New Ibadan, a popular tourist destination. The *Coldstar* fled but was severely damaged, crash landing on Oota Mheen, where 1,017 lives were lost. Eyewitness accounts give conflicting reports on the identity of the attackers. To date, no known piracy group or other entity has claimed responsibility for the attack.

Original designation: SL Orion. Built by: Fortran Corporation. Construction site: Heliodome Shipyards. Keel in Orbit: EE 9239. Launched: EE 9241. Engine Type: Twin Genero-2600 Needle Drives. Capacity: 60,100 passengers, 8,100 crew. Full Technical Specifications Available Upon Request.

VOL. 683.472

HYPERCUBE: A hypercube is the equivalent of a square that exists in more than one dimension. For example, a square in three dimensions is a cube, while a square in four dimensions is a tesseract, and a square in five dimensions is a pentaract or 5-cube, and so on.

VOL. 2800.001–2956.080

INSPINITY: Inspinity, also known as M-space, is the primary method by which most starships travel the galaxy at velocities that appear to exceed the speed of light, although in reality this fundamental law of physics is never broken. An infinite number of multiple universes coexist with our universe, occupying the same space as our own, but each existing in their own enclosed dimension and cut off from ours. However, with the invention of the Needle Drive, it has become possible to use these other universes to shorten the distance between two points. When a ship in our universe wishes to travel between two points, Needle Drives search for alternate universes where these two points sit very close together and then tunnel through that universe to make use of the shorter route. The ship then pops back into our universe when it arrives safely at its destination. This mode of travel is sometimes called threading the needle. It is interesting to note that sometimes, natural phenomena can cause one universe to temporarily leak into another. In ancient times, these instances were often mistakenly attributed to ghosts.

VOL. 3901.003

INTERSTELLAR COMMUNICATIONS NETWORK: Unlike thousands of years ago when humans used something called radio, communications in the Exodussic Age are instantaneous, thanks to the invention of Q-comms, often simply referred to as comms. Modern communications do not require a signal and are not limited by the speed of light. The technology utilizes a quirk in physics called entanglement, whereby two particles can be a billion light-years distant from each other, yet can still affect each other–at exactly the same time. The result is that when a message is transmitted using this technology, it arrives at the exact moment that it is sent, sometimes sooner. Entanglement is a delicate state for particles to occupy indefinitely and these systems require constant monitoring and protection. The network of Q-nodes that are deployed throughout the galaxy to relay communications allows for near-limitless route handling, resulting in a system that can rarely be disrupted.

VOL. 3978.000

JARANJAR: Jaranjars, also known as tiger-apes, are a species of tree-dwelling carnivore native to the jungles of Oota Mheen. Jaranjars have a striking coat of silver-and-black stripes and a remarkably long prehensile tail, which they use to catch and strangle unsuspecting prey. Many anthropologists frown upon using the term tiger-ape, since apes do not have tails.

VOL. 4195.050

JUBA: Juba is a tidally locked planet in the Selenium System, and is an independent star nation. Juba's primary industry is as a refueling stop for intergalactic trade; however, it has expanded its role as a small trading hub in recent years. Juba's capital city is Vespertine, with an estimated population of 31 million.
VOL. 4385.009

OOTA MHEEN: Oota Mheen is the second planet in the Mheen system, orbiting a type of star known as a red dwarf. This ancient star type is small and not very luminous. Although daylight appears bright on the planet's surface, the sunlight is in fact significantly weaker than that found in other star systems. Plant life has evolved on Oota Mheen to absorb as much sunlight as possible, consequently many varieties appear black to human eyes. Oota Mheen's high temperatures are due to geothermal activity.
VOL. 40998.897

THUNDERHEADS: Thunderheads are a class of advanced airborne troop common to most military structures across the galaxy. Thunderheads can deploy from low altitude all the way up to suborbital flight. They use boosters traditionally known as rocket packs to control and direct their descent. Once on the ground, booster packs are discarded, since they do not hold enough power to get a trooper airborne again. Thunderheads vary widely

in their skills and abilities from star nation to star nation. For example, the much-feared Thunderheads of Kutch are known as the Red Devils for their striking red uniforms and their ruthlessness with their enemies, while the Thunderheads of Tooba serve mostly ceremonial functions.
VOL. 51027.744

TRAP-BLOOM: Any one of a number of carnivorous plant species that have emerged on several worlds. Trap-blooms remain open for days or weeks at a time until prey cross their petals, triggering the bloom to snap shut, whereupon it consumes its prey. The Venus flytrap of Earth is one such example. The largest trap-bloom ever recorded was found on Gada Rentis and measured 47.3 paces across. It was capable of trapping and ingesting up to three large trabasaurs at once.
VOL. 52207.233

YANTI: Yantis are a two-legged trabasaur often used for travel and home-defense purposes. Yantis come in various colors; the most common is sandy brown. Their coat consists of patches of feathers, which can easily fall out, leaving significant bald spots. Their beaks feature needlelike teeth, which can cause significant damage to their prey.
VOL. 98303.102